Bedford Falls: The Story Continues

Anne Morse

Copyright 2014 by Joanne Gail Morse

Cover design by Rachael Sinclair

Back cover photo: *It's a Wonderful Life*, 1946, Paramount

All rights reserved. No part of this book may be reproduced in any form or by any electronic or mechanical means including information storage and retrieval systems, without permission from the author.

ISBN 978-1505357509

Printed in the United States of America

First Printing: November 2014

Anne Morse may be contacted at `AnneGailMorse@gmail.com`

For my husband, Brent

Bailey Family Tree Continued

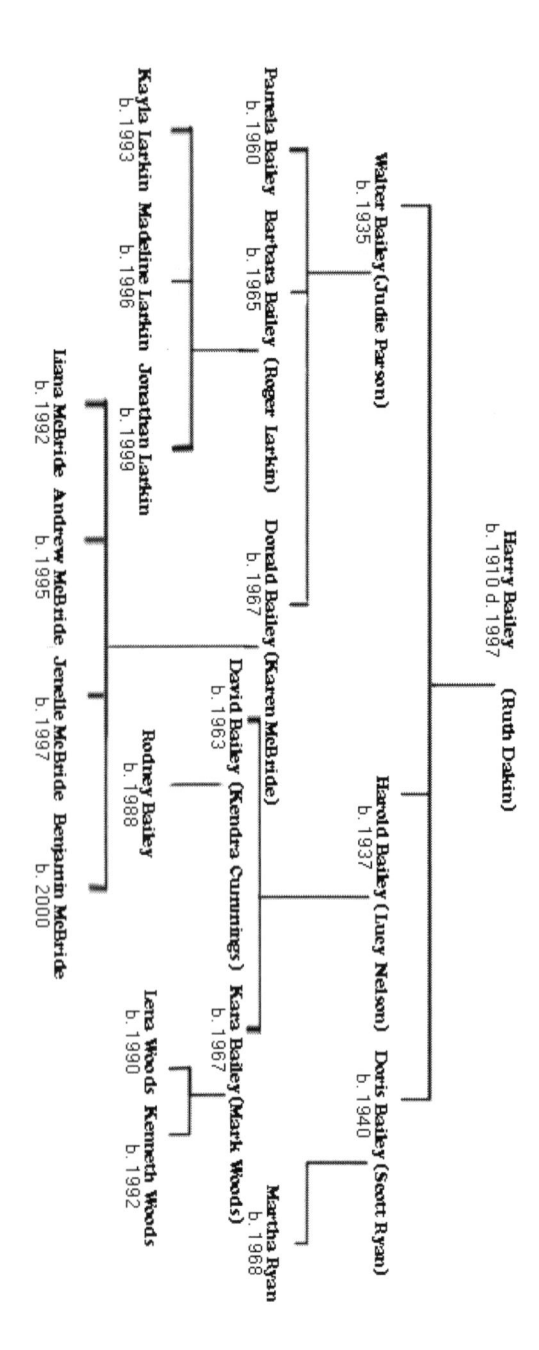

Harry Bailey b. 1910 d. 1997 — (Ruth Dakin)

- **Walter Bailey (Judie Parson)** b. 1935
  - **Pamela Bailey** b. 1960
  - **Barbara Bailey (Roger Larkin)** b. 1965
    - Kayla Larkin b. 1993
    - Madeleine Larkin b. 1996
    - Jonathan Larkin b. 1999
  - **Donald Bailey** b. 1967
- **Harold Bailey (Lucy Nelson)** b. 1937
  - **David Bailey (Karen McBride)** b. 1963
    - Iiana McBride b. 1992
    - Andrew McBride b. 1995
    - Jenelle McBride b. 1997
    - Benjamin McBride b. 2000
  - **Rodney Bailey** b. 1988
  - **Kara Bailey (Mark Woods)** b. 1967
    - Lena Woods b. 1990
    - Kenneth Woods b. 1992
- **Doris Bailey (Scott Ryan)** b. 1940
  - Martha Ryan b. 1968

Bailey Family Tree

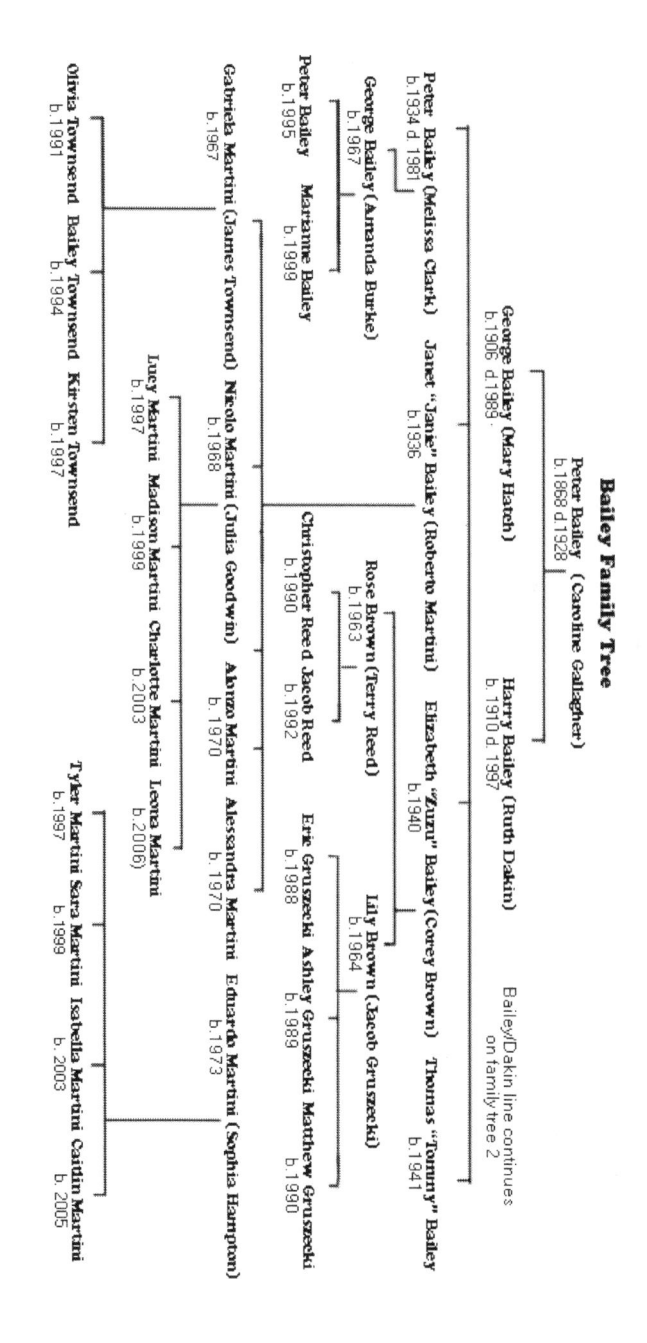

Peter Bailey (Caroline Gallagher)
b.1868 d.1928

- **George Bailey (Mary Hatch)** b.1906 d.1989
- **Harry Bailey (Ruth Dakin)** b.1910 d.1997

Bailey/Dakin line continues on family tree 2

George Bailey (Mary Hatch) descendants

- **Peter Bailey (Melissa Clark)** b.1934 d.1981
  - **George Bailey (Amanda Burke)** b.1967
    - **Peter Bailey** b.1995
    - **Marianne Bailey** b.1999
- **Janet "Janie" Bailey (Roberto Martini)** b.1936
  - **Gabriela Martini (James Townsend)** b.1967
    - **Olivia Townsend** b.1991
    - **Bailey Townsend** b.1994
    - **Kirsten Townsend** b.1997
  - **Nicolo Martini (Julia Goodwin)** b.1968
    - **Christopher Reed** b.1990
    - **Jacob Reed** b.1992
      - **Rose Brown (Terry Reed)** b.1963
    - **Lucy Martini** b.1997
    - **Madison Martini** b.1999
    - **Charlotte Martini** b.2003
    - **Leona Martini** b.2006
  - **Abruzo Martini** b.1970
  - **Alessandra Martini** b.1970
  - **Eduardo Martini (Sophia Hampton)** b.1973
    - **Tyler Martini** b.1997
    - **Sara Martini** b.1999
    - **Isabella Martini** b.2003
    - **Caitlin Martini** b.2005
- **Elizabeth "Zuzu" Bailey (Corey Brown)** b.1940
  - **Rose Brown (Terry Reed)** b.1963
  - **Lily Brown (Jacob Gruszecki)** b.1964
    - **Eric Gruszecki** b.1988
    - **Ashley Gruszecki** b.1989
    - **Matthew Gruszecki** b.1990
- **Thomas "Tommy" Bailey** b.1941

Hatch Family Tree

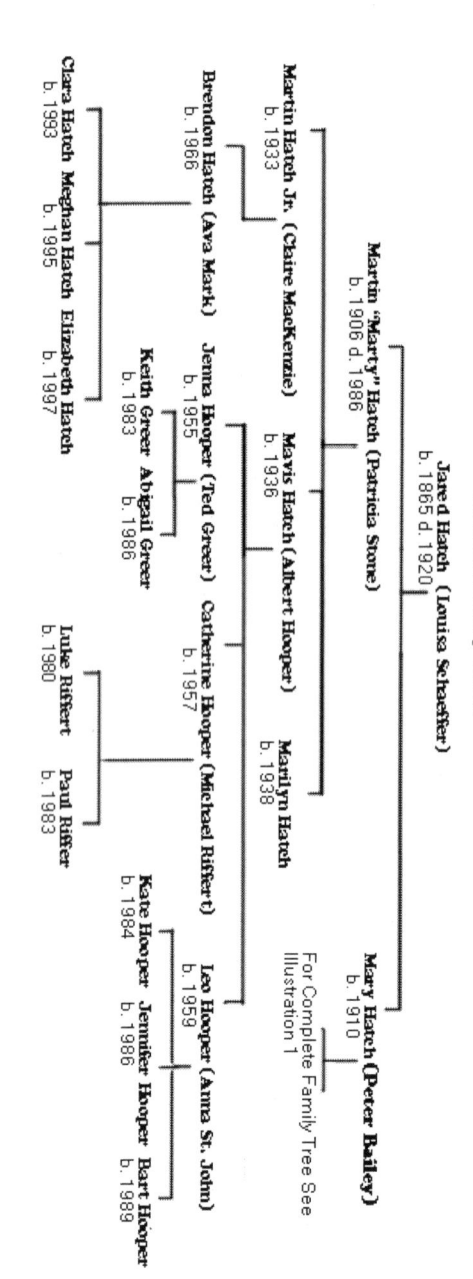

Jared Hatch (Louisa Schaeffer)
b. 1865 d. 1920

- Martin "Marty" Hatch (Patricia Stone)
  b. 1906 d. 1986
  - Martin Hatch Jr. (Claire MacKenzie)
    b. 1933
    - Brendon Hatch (Ava Mark)
      b. 1966
      - Clara Hatch b. 1993
      - Meghan Hatch b. 1995
      - Elizabeth Hatch b. 1997
  - Mavis Hatch (Albert Hooper)
    b. 1936
    - Jenna Hooper (Ted Greer)
      b. 1955
      - Keith Greer b. 1983
      - Abigail Greer b. 1986
    - Catherine Hooper (Michael Riffert)
      b. 1957
      - Luke Riffert b. 1980
      - Paul Riffert b. 1983
    - Leo Hooper (Anna St. John)
      b. 1959
      - Kate Hooper b. 1984
      - Jennifer Hooper b. 1986
      - Bart Hooper b. 1989
  - Marilyn Hatch
    b. 1938
- Mary Hatch (Peter Bailey)
  b. 1910

For Complete Family Tree See Illustration 1

"For what will it profit a man if he gains the whole world and forfeits his own soul?"

– Jesus
(Matthew 16:26)

Prologue

Christmas Eve, 2007

"Hello, Joseph. Trouble?"

"Yes, sir. Looks like we'll have to send someone down. A man named George Bailey is in trouble."

"Didn't we already send someone down to help him? Right after the Second World War?"

"This is his grandson, sir."

"Oh, I see. How many people have been praying?"

Joseph looked uncomfortable. "Just one, sir."

"One! You want to send someone down on Christmas Eve because one person is praying?"

"She's one of our most faithful saints, sir. And she's been praying all afternoon for her grandson."

"All right, if you say so. Whose turn is it?"

"It's that clock-maker's turn again."

"Oh, yes, Clarence. Isn't he the one we sent to help George Bailey's grandfather?"

"That's right, sir. His methods were a bit unorthodox, but he got the job done."

The heavens rumbled with holy laughter. "That's right, he did. Earned his wings that night, didn't he?"

"That's right, sir."

"All right, Joseph. Send for Clarence. By the way, why is nobody praying for George Bailey except his grandmother?"

"Because," Joseph responded, "Everybody else hates him."

Friday, December 14, 2007

Chapter 1

George Peter Bailey stepped through the glass doors of Bailey Investments on Fifth Avenue, his cashmere coat wrapped snugly around his tall figure. Rain was pouring down hard; there was no hint of the promised snow.

The doorman, recognizing the company CEO, lifted an umbrella over his head. "Evening, Mr. Bailey," he murmured.

"Good evening, William," George responded, his eyes darting up and down the street. No demonstrators tonight, thank God. George's limousine and driver were waiting at the curb. William walked George to the car and swung open the door. George bent his frame into the limo's warm, leather interior, and William closed the door behind him.

"Evening, Mr. Bailey," his driver greeted him cheerfully. "Straight home tonight?"

"That's right, Adrian."

Ten days before Christmas, New York City sparkled with thousands of lights. Skyscrapers were festooned with enormous, red-ribboned wreaths; department store windows offered visions of the best Christmas money could buy. Crowds of late afternoon shoppers fought for sidewalk space with office workers trying to get home.

The city throbbed with the energy of Christmas. But it was a hard, bright, cold energy.

George saw and felt none of it. As Adrian wove the limo expertly through the slick city streets, George's mind was focused exclusively on the difficulties he faced over the next few days, particularly those involving the old McClure building.

Bailey Investments had purchased the vacant McClure apartment building on Vestry Street in Tribeca three years ago for thirty million. George had expected to spend an additional ten to twelve million restoring it and upgrading the small apartments into larger, more luxurious ones. But the expense of rewiring, replacing rotting walls and floors, and updating plumbing had skyrocketed above the estimates – in part to meet the latest "green" demands. George had called the contractor personally, his voice as cold as his chilly blue eyes, telling him to keep costs down – or else. A few tenants had moved in on the sixth and seventh floors, but Bailey Investments would not begin to make real money until renovation on was complete on the remaining floors.

Even worse was the situation with the Trent Towers property, also in Tribeca, which Bailey Investments had purchased two years before. George's company planned to turn the first floor into retail shopping space and convert the aging apartments into sleek, multimillion-dollar ones. The problem was, Trent Towers had been filled with elderly tenants who had lived there for decades. They'd kicked up a fuss when Bailey Investments notified them that they would have to be out of their apartments by December 31. Several had challenged their evictions. Bailey Investments' lawyers had finally and successfully dealt with all the court cases. But now, a community action group had sprung up, led by a media-savvy activist who invited television news reporters to interview some of the more elderly residents, who cried on cue (George thought cynically) about how they had nowhere else to go. Bailey Investments had refused to back down, but the activists hadn't given up their goal of getting the company to allow the oldest renters, at least, to live out their lives in their apartments, and had been waving protest signs in front of Bailey Investments nearly every day. In the end, as the deadline approached, most of them had reluctantly complied. But there were a few holdouts.

The rain lashed against the limo's windows. A traffic light turned green, and Adrian inched the car forward. "Where you gonna spend Christmas, Mr. Bailey?" Adrian asked.

George's handsome face hardened slightly. "In Vermont, skiing," he replied briefly. Here was another fine mess, he thought. His wife, Amanda, was determined to go to Bedford Falls for Christmas this year, even though George had accepted an invitation to spend the holidays skiing with important business contacts. Even if the invitation had not existed, George reflected, he did not want to go to Bedford Falls. The town bored him. All small towns did. He much preferred having the families visit *them*, in the city, where there was so much to do.

But Amanda, unexpectedly, had proven stubborn, and last night they'd had a colossal row. They'd not spoken this morning, and George was not looking forward to arriving home tonight. Especially since – George cursed under his breath – half a dozen community activists were waiting in front of his home, a glass penthouse duplex perched dramatically atop an art deco loft building on Hudson Street, which had set George back $45 million. A shout went up as they spotted his car, and they began waving their homemade signs.

"Hey, George! How many people are you going to put on the streets tonight?"

"Hey, George, how about giving poor folks a break?"

An older woman took a more pleading tone. "Mr. Bailey, imagine if these folks were your parents. How would you feel if someone threw *them* out on the street?"

George ignored them all. The doorman opened his car door and held an umbrella over George's head as he strode from the curb to the building. The doorman quickly pulled open the front door and George entered the lobby, shaking the rain from his briefcase onto the highly polished hardwood floor with its striking geometric design. As the door swung shut behind him, George caught the final insult:

"Have a lovely evening, Bailey – in your nice, warm duplex!"

George punched the elevator button for the top floor. As the elevator shot to the top, George wondered again what kind of mood Amanda would be in, and how quickly she could be put into a better one if she was still upset about Christmas.

Tonight they were among the guests of honor at a party celebrating the purchase of a Picasso for New York's Castlebury Museum of Art. George and Amanda had written a $10 million check toward its purchase. Everyone who was anyone would be at tonight's dinner dance and fundraiser at the museum. George – who had been invited to unveil the Picasso – did not intend to miss it, and he did not intend for his wife to miss it, either.

Chapter 2

$\mathcal{L}$ike his grandfather and namesake, George Bailey was born dying to get out of Bedford Falls. Unlike his grandfather, he succeeded.

Ironically, his success had come, in part, from the very man who had almost singlehandedly destroyed the first George Bailey's dreams of leaving the small town where he'd been born, some 265 miles northwest of New York City, and building skyscrapers: Henry F. Potter, the richest and meanest man in town. Old Man Potter had died in 1946, a few months after that remarkable Christmas when George's grandfather had contemplated throwing himself into the Bedford River.

"Why did you do that?" five-year-old George, curled up on his grandfather's lap at the old Bailey house on Sycamore Street, had asked.

"Because I thought I was worth more dead than alive," his grandfather replied.

"Were you?"

"Nobody is worth more dead than alive," Grandfather had said firmly, pushing back a lock of white hair. He was seated in an ancient, chintz-covered chair, his long legs resting on a matching ottoman. "Now, pipe down, George, and listen."

George had listened, fascinated, to the story of an angel who had come down from heaven on Christmas Eve to help his grandfather realize that he had lived a truly worthwhile life – even a great life – even if he hadn't built skyscrapers a hundred stories high and bridges a mile long, as he'd dreamed. The little boy was especially intrigued by his grandfather's vision of what the world would have been like if he'd never been born. Playing with a miniature replica of the Bailey Building and Loan and swinging his short legs, George wondered aloud how different the world would have been if *he* had never been born.

"There wouldn't be that broken pane in the Gowers' window," his mother pointed out. "And the snowman the Martini children built would still be standing."

The aunts and uncles and cousins, gathered at George and Mary Bailey's home for Christmas of 1972, laughed. Young George scowled in annoyance. Even at age five, he hadn't liked being teased. But his grandfather had smiled his slow smile and hugged George closer.

"If you'd never been born, I wouldn't be sitting here telling you stories. And your grandmother would not have made these cookies," he added, as Mary Bailey came into the living room with a plate of warm snickerdoodles and mugs of hot chocolate. George immediately hopped down, snatched three of the cookies, and stuffed them into his mouth, relishing the rich confection of butter, cinnamon, and sugar.

"Don't be so greedy, darling," Grandmother Mary scolded gently, ruffling her grandson's blond hair.

George climbed back onto his grandfather's lap. "Tell me about Great-Grandpa and Great Uncle Billy," he ordered.

"What was that?" Grandfather asked. "Don't forget, I'm deaf in one ear, and the other one isn't working too well, either."

It was a story George was already familiar with, but he liked hearing it again. He knew his great-grandfather Peter Bailey had left a New York City tenement in 1903 with his brother Billy and settled in Bedford Falls, leaving behind their Irish immigrant parents and four younger siblings. The two brothers had started up the Bailey Brothers Building and Loan Association not long afterward.

Peter Bailey had married Caroline Gallaher and the couple had become parents to two sons, George and Harry. Two cousins, Tilly and Eustace, arrived from New York a few years later; Peter and Billy had given them both jobs in the Building and Loan.

George knew his grandfather was deaf in one ear because he'd caught a bad cold during the winter of 1919 after throwing himself into the icy Bedford River to rescue his little brother Harry. Nine years later, great-grandfather Peter Bailey had died of a stroke the evening before Grandfather had planned to work his way to Europe aboard a cattle boat. Grandfather had canceled his trip in order to bury his father, comfort his mother, and straighten out affairs at the Building and Loan, which his Uncle Billy had managed to get into a mess almost before his brother was cold.

And then, just as Grandfather was about to leave for college, the board of directors of the Building and Loan announced that unless he stayed on to run the place, they would shut it down, as Henry Potter was urging them to do.

"That's when you yelled at Old Man Potter, isn't it?" George asked with relish. He fished a penny out of his grandfather's vest pocket and dropped it into his toy bank. "He wanted to close the Building and Loan. You called him a warped, frustrated old man."

His grandfather grinned reminiscently. "That's right, I did."

Grandfather had reluctantly agreed to stay on at the Building and Loan, knowing he was giving up forever his chance at a college education and the exciting life he'd dreamed of. It turned out to be a providential decision for Bedford Fallsians, however, when the stock market crashed a year later, signaling the start of the Great Depression. Hundreds of local men lost their jobs, including many young fathers; few could continue making regular payments on their homes. Grandfather had refused to foreclose on them despite the hardship this had imposed on the Building and Loan and on Grandfather personally.

The bleakness of Grandfather's life lifted considerably when he wed a Bedford Falls girl named Mary Hatch in 1932, after a courtship that had hiccupped along for several years. The young couple moved into the old Granville House at 132 Sycamore after paying off the back taxes. Four children were born to them: George's father, Peter Bailey; Aunt Janie; Uncle Tommy; and Aunt Elizabeth, whom grandfather had nicknamed Zuzu, after the little clown the National Biscuit Company put on its boxes of gingersnaps.

George knew that Great-Uncle Harry, a heroic Navy pilot during World War II, had being awarded the Congressional Medal of Honor. But Grandfather remained stuck in Bedford Falls, rejected from active duty on account of his bad ear (and, Grandfather always suspected, possibly because Old Man Potter, as head of the draft board, wanted to keep him in Bedford Falls out of sheer spite). Grandfather, though disappointed over not being able to take a more active role in the war, put aside his frustration and became an air raid warden. He continued to develop Bailey Park, which allowed the town's poor immigrant families to move out of Potter's shacks and into decent homes.

And then, as the family was joyfully awaiting Harry's arrival home on Christmas Eve of 1945, the Great Crisis struck. Grandfather's Uncle Billy had somehow managed to lose $8,000 of the Building and Loan Association's money – an enormous sum in those days. By a fateful coincidence, the bank examiner happened to arrive that afternoon.

This disaster, on top of so many years of strain, struggle, and disappointment, had driven George Bailey to the brink of suicide. Desperate and a little drunk from those highballs he'd downed at Martini's Place, Grandfather had rammed his car into a tree a stone's throw from the bridge that spanned the Bedford River.

And then, just as Grandfather was contemplating ending his life so that Mary would at least have the insurance money, an angel named Clarence Oddbody had appeared. Clarence had had the bright idea of showing Grandfather what the town would have been like if George hadn't been around. Lovely little Bedford Falls would have been transformed into Pottersville, complete with bars, strip clubs, and angry, depressed, and violent people. His children didn't exist, and Mary was an old maid working at the library.

And then Grandfather, realizing for the first time that he had truly lived a wonderful life, and appreciating how rich he actually was, had prayed, "Clarence! Get me back to my wife and kids! Please, God, I want to live again!"

By the time he was nine, George no longer believed elements of his grandfather's tale. He'd probably been knocked unconscious when his car had struck the tree, and dreamed up the dimwitted angel. Or maybe it was hitting his head on the floor of Martini's Place after Mr. Walsh, the schoolteacher's husband, decked him for insulting his wife.

All anyone knew for sure was that Bert O'Brien, the town policeman, had found Grandfather standing on the bridge, talking to himself and behaving strangely. When George arrived back home he was still behaving oddly, but according to Grandmother Mary, he'd also been tremendously excited. He'd hugged her and the kids over and over again, murmuring "Thank you God. Thank you Clarence." The townspeople, learning of the missing money, had donated enough cash to cover the loss. The fate of the missing $8000 remained a mystery.

Everyone in Bedford Falls noticed the remarkable change in George Bailey after that night. He took more pleasure in his family, his friends, and even his job, which he'd always loathed. He no longer yearned to get out of Bedford Falls, or seemed to think that life had cruelly passed him by. Life exhilarated George Bailey for the first time since he was a boy, reading the *National Geographic* behind the counter at Mr. Gower's drugstore and dreaming of becoming an explorer.

George frequently took evening strolls through Bailey Park, greeting newcomers, patting dogs, and pausing to chat with old friends as they worked in their gardens. George even went out of his way to be kind to Old Man Potter, waving to him in the street and cheerfully shouting, "Hello there, Mr. Potter! How's life treating you?"

Potter, who'd been an old man even when Grandfather was a boy, was sick now. He had begun to shrink physically from the powerfully built man that he'd been to a shriveled, shaky scarecrow.

Something about Christmas of 1945, when the old man had failed in his attempt to have his nemesis thrown in jail for misappropriation of funds, seemed to have altered Potter, too. Grandfather thought he knew the answer. For more than forty years Potter's chief diversion in life had been attempting to beat the Bailey family and shut down the Building and Loan, just about the only business in Bedford Falls he didn't control. He'd done his best to destroy the Baileys and everything they valued. It was clear now that he would never succeed. Despite all the underhanded tricks he'd played on the Baileys over the years, that piddling little Building and Loan, run by two generations of Bailey chumps, was still open for business, still building homes for lazy rabble (as Potter viewed them) – immigrants who found their way to Bedford Falls from New York City.

Everybody still called Potter the meanest man in town, but somehow, Potter's heart wasn't in his meanness anymore. He stopped waving his stick at children to frighten them off, and no longer made contemptuous comments about the town's poor, ignorant "garlic eaters." When he felt strong enough, Potter had his longtime bodyguard drive him to the bank. There, he huddled next to the heater, trying to stay warm, and feebly ordered people about – people who increasingly ignored him.

In the end, Potter's heart failed, which surprised the town because nobody in Bedford Falls believed Potter actually *had* a heart. His bodyguard found him dead in his wheelchair at home, in front of an open safe, wads of cash scattered about the floor. Nobody attended Potter's funeral – nobody, that is, except George Bailey.

A few days later came the biggest surprise to hit Bedford Falls in twenty years. Potter, incredibly, had left his entire estate to George Bailey. While George was just as big a chump as his father and uncle (Potter wrote), he was, nevertheless, the only man who'd ever managed to best him, "and as I once told you a long time ago, that takes some doing."

Besides, there was nobody else to leave his fortune to. As far as anyone knew, Potter had no family. He had no charitable interests and no community spirit, as he'd spent eighty-four years proving. And perhaps he wanted to find out, from wherever he was now, if having all that money would finally corrupt his arch-rival.

The entire town erupted with joy over George's unexpected inheritance, and then waited to see what he would do with it. The first thing George did was to take Mary on a honeymoon that had been delayed for fourteen years. They took the train to New York City, spent three days in the Waldorf Hotel bridal suite filled with flowers and "the oldest champagne, the richest caviar, the hottest music and the prettiest wife," as George enthusiastically put it, and then traveled to Europe, not on a cattle boat, as George had once planned to do, but aboard the *Queen Mary*, newly refitted after the war, leaving their children in the care of Grandmother Bailey and Grandmother Hatch.

When they reached Paris, George draped Mary in the loveliest clothes she'd ever possessed: hats, gowns, shoes, stockings, gloves, and a luxurious mink coat. He bought her expensive perfume and an emerald-and-diamond bracelet with earrings to match. For her birthday, George gave Mary a moonstone pendent, in memory of his promise, made as they walked home from the high school dance in 1928, to lasso the moon for her.

The couple visited London – still terribly bomb-damaged from the war – and floated down the canals of Venice on a gondola, where George read his own corny poems to Mary by moonlight. They wandered through the Bordeaux region of France, sampling wines, watched the running of the bulls in Barcelona, and prayed prayers of thanksgiving in the churches of Rome.

George saw everything he'd longed to see as a young man, but it meant much more now, visiting these exciting cities with Mary at his side. Three months later, the Baileys came home, sun-tanned and deeply happy. And then, George got busy.

First, he hired away from one of the biggest banks in New York a clever and trustworthy young man named Jonathan Lawrence to run the Building and Loan. Lawrence had grown tired of the pace and grime of big city life, and was eager to eager to bring his young family to live in the small, friendly town they'd discovered while vacationing in upstate New York.

George became a board member of the Building and Loan, keeping a close eye on Lawrence's decisions, but otherwise having little to do with day-to-day affairs. Uncle Billy, the two agreed, should be pensioned off and left to enjoy his old age. The cheerful old man spent the remainder of his life wandering about the town with his pet raven, often stopping in for a drink at Martini's Place, telling anyone who would listen about the grand old days when the Baileys had crossed swords with Old Man Potter, and singing Irish ballads.

Next, George and Mary enthusiastically turned their attention to remodeling the old Granville house – now the old Bailey house – adding central heating and air-conditioning, and replacing the last few windows on the unused top floor that the couple had broken that long-ago night of Mary's graduation dance. They repainted and bought furniture, draperies, and carpets. But for some reason, George never repaired the knob atop the newel post at the foot of the stairs in the front hall. That loose knob seemed to mean something special to George.

And then, George began to build things. He built a low-cost medical clinic for the town's poor – a godsend when polio struck in the 1950s – and named it after Robert Gower, the son of his druggist friend, Emil Gower, who'd died in a flu epidemic many years before.

George funded repairs to Bedford Falls Presbyterian Church, where he had wept and prayed on V-E Day and V-J Day, marking the great victories against Germany and Japan. He turned Old Man Potter's mansion into a comfortable assisted living home for the town's elderly – many of whose children had died in one of the nation's wars, or during the flu epidemic, or during the diphtheria epidemic in the twenties, and had no one else to look after them.

In honor of his mother, who died in 1954, George designed the Caroline Gallaher Bailey Memorial Gardens in Bailey Park, planting many of the tulips, roses, and hydrangea bushes himself. At its center, George designed a memorial to those who had died in the First and Second World Wars, later adding the names of those who'd perished in Korea and Vietnam. He made sure the town's war widows and orphans were not neglected.

With the town's approval, George erected a statue of his father in front of the Building and Loan.

It seemed right to spend Potter's money on projects that benefited the people of Bedford Falls. After all, Potter had stolen so much from them.

As the decades passed, and George's hair began to turn white, nothing delighted him more than outfoxing would-be Henry Potters who tried to make their fortunes at the expense of the good of Bedford Falls. For instance, when the owner of the local Bijou retired and put the theater up for sale in the 1960s, a theater chain known for showing "R" and "X" rated films made an offer. Hearing of this, George promptly bought the theater himself. He then handed it over to the town on condition that only films suitable for families be shown there. If people wanted to see other types of films, they could go to New York City.

During the same decade, when a big drugstore chain tried to move into Bedford Falls, threatening to put Gower Drugs – now being run by a Gower great-nephew – out of business, George convinced the town leaders to refuse to give them a zoning permit. While legal wrangling went on over this, George encouraged the townspeople to begin a mail campaign to the drugstore chain's corporate headquarters, telling it that Bedford Falls didn't need another pharmacy, and that if the company insisted on moving in, nobody in Bedford Falls would patronize it. The company canceled its plans.

When a developer wanted to throw up rows of cheap houses and apartments, George sent them packing. And when the 1960s brought civil rights unrest, George quietly funded college scholarships for every black graduate of Bedford Falls High School. Because so many Bedford Fallsians admired George, they followed his leadership in this matter, as they had in so many previous ones. Consequently, racial unrest was kept to a minimum, and many of the recipients of George's generosity eventually returned to the town. Among them was Richard Baldwin, a great-nephew of the Bailey family's maid, Annie Perkins. Dr. Baldwin became the county's first black physician.

As George and Mary's four children grew into teenagers in the 1950s, they took their own turn at the fountain at Gower Drugs, serving root beer floats and cherry Cokes to friends who shoved dimes into the noisy new jukebox and jitterbugged the afternoons away. One by one, the Bailey children graduated from high school. And then, to George's deep satisfaction, Pete, Janie, Zuzu, and Tommy each departed for college, madly waving goodbye to their parents from the window of the train as it snorted and rolled away from Bedford Falls.

Pete attended Rensselaer Polytechnic Institute and became the engineer his father had longed to become. He built an international reputation for the sleek elegance of the office buildings he designed. In 1963, he married Melissa Clark, the daughter of a London banker, and in 1967, the couple gave George his first grandchild: George Peter Bailey, named for his father, grandfather, and great-grandfather.

Janie, who had shown musical gifts from early childhood, attended the Julliard School and became a concert pianist. Her home base was New York City, but Janie returned frequently to Bedford Falls to visit her family and entertain at community events. During a 1966 visit, at a potluck picnic celebrating her father's 60th birthday, Janie could not help noticing how handsome her old school chum, Roberto Martini, had become.

In 1967, after working out religious differences (their children would attend both Protestant and Catholic churches, they decided), Janie and Roberto were married. Janie cut down on her performance schedule while Roberto, who had attended culinary school, served as executive chef at the revamped Martini's Place. Five children were eventually born to the couple.

Janie was now seventy-one years old and retired. But she still performed frequently at the Presbyterian Church and at local festivities. And she spent much of her time enjoying her eleven grandchildren, who liked nothing more than helping out their grandfather and uncles in the family restaurant.

Zuzu attended Boston Architectural College, graduating with a degree in landscape design. Like her mother, Zuzu had no interest in living life on a grand scale. All she wanted was to return to Bedford Falls, marry, and have a family – which is exactly what she did. She married an artist named Corey Slater Brown – literally the boy next door – when she was twenty-three, and gave birth to two daughters, Rose and Lily. She designed gardens and parks in and around Bedford Falls. (At her father's suggestion, she called her business "Zuzu's Petals.") When out-of-town concerts called her sister Janie away, Zuzu looked after her children, who adored Aunt Zuzu.

As for Tommy Bailey, George and Mary's youngest child, he did not seem to be able to follow through on his goals. Less academic than his brother and sisters, Tommy struggled through math and science courses in high school. His father had hired a tutor for him, but even so, Tommy had graduated near the bottom of his class.

Tommy began studies at a regional college, but left after just one year – not, as he told his parents, because he'd lost interest, but because he'd been kicked out for failing grades, the result of too much partying and too little studying. Not knowing what to do with himself, and longing to get out of Bedford Falls, he'd joined the army, serving in Korea just after the war. Hating the cold, along with the discipline of army life, Tommy gladly re-entered civilian life after two years.

In the 1960s, Tommy worked sporadically, mostly in construction, and experimented a bit with drugs. Like Uncle Billy, he drank too much. When he ran out of money, which he frequently did, Tommy moved back in with his parents, who loved him but despaired of his ever making something of his life.

As a member of the town council, George encouraged the building of light industry on the outskirts of town, including a software development firm, giving newcomers a place to work. And as the decades passed, immigrants from Western Europe gave way to arrivals from Eastern Europe, Asia, Africa, and Central America. George and Mary delighted in greeting these new families and making sure they had a decent place to live.

As it always had done, the Building and Loan gave loans to people the bank turned down, and refused to throw families out of their homes if they were temporarily unable to make their mortgage payments. Very seldom did the Building and Loan regret its decisions.

George and Mary spent much happy time with their eight grandchildren – George, Zuzu's two daughters, and Janie's gang of five – most of whom lived in Bedford Falls. The only great-grandchild George Bailey lived to see was Peter Bailey, the son of George and Amanda.

As the town prospered, larger and more luxurious homes were built for the bankers and businessmen, and later, for software engineers. And so life went on in Bedford Falls much as it always had, with George Bailey keeping a sharp eye out for anyone who might damage what he and his father had sacrificed so much to build.

*****

George Bailey's happiness was grievously dimmed when his son Pete and his wife Melissa were killed in a plane crash in 1981, when they were traveling from Singapore to San Francisco to oversee construction on a building Pete had designed. Fourteen-year-old Geroge had stayed in Singapore with friends of his parents because he wanted to attend a party. He was brought back to Bedford Falls, the place of his birth, by his sorrowing grandparents. Zuzu and Janie would happily have taken young George in, but his grandfather firmly declared that he wanted to look after the boy himself.

As his eldest grandson and namesake grew from adolescence into young manhood, his grandfather worried about him. The boy had been deeply affected by the loss of his parents, and to a great extent had withdrawn into himself.

Young George was tall, handsome, ambitious, and intelligent, like his grandfather. But unlike his sociable grandfather, George was reserved, watchful, and silent. He was also restless, his grandfather realized. The boy had loved traveling the world with his parents as his father designed and built one skyscraper after another. Realizing this, George had taken his grandson to Australia when the boy was sixteen, just the two of them.

Young George had seemed more cheerful after that. But as the years went by, he seemed less and less interested in his family or the town. When he was accepted at Yale, he was as eager to get out of Bedford Falls – essentially for good – as his grandfather had once been. After graduating *summa cum laude*, George attended the Wharton Business School.

He spent his summer vacations working at the Building and Loan and learned something about the banking business. In many ways, George and Mary were pleased with how young George had turned out. But during the summer of his twentieth year, he had horrified his grandparents by making a decision of breathtaking selfishness.

Chapter 3

Amanda Burke Bailey sat at her dressing table, pinning up her blonde hair. The fundraiser was still three hours away, but she wanted to arrive early in order to help out with any last-minute problems.

It would also be an excuse for avoiding George a bit longer. He usually arrived around 6:30 p.m., unless a crisis, large or small, kept him in the office.

Her husband had risen, showered, and dressed for work that morning without a word to her. Thinking of their argument of the night before, Amanda sighed. Their conflict over where to spend Christmas was merely the latest in a long series of fights that had led to ominous cracks in their fourteen-year marriage.

Amanda had been dismayed at George's decision to evict long-time residents of the McClure building. But when she'd brought it up a few weeks before, George had become angry; he disliked her "meddling" in his business affairs.

They'd also had serious disagreements about the children, twelve-year-old Peter and seven-year-old Marianne. George had promised to attend his daughter's Christmas play, in which Marianne had a substantial role. But when the curtain rose, George was not in the audience. Marianne had said her lines perfectly, but when parents came backstage to congratulate their kids at the play's conclusion, Marianne's happy face had crumpled when she saw only her mother. George didn't even remember the play had taken place when he arrived home that evening, tired after flying to and from Albany, where he'd lunched with the governor. Marianne, waiting impatiently for her father to ask about her performance, had finally burst into tears and run to her room.

"She'll get over it," George had said when Amanda had filled him in.

Amanda was furious. "She'll *never* forget about this! You should have been there!"

George had wearily told her to leave him alone, and gone into his study to pour himself a drink.

He'd made it up with Marianne later, but Amanda noticed, in the following weeks, that the little girl looked at her father in a different way. Her eyes seemed more cautious, and when she won an award at school just before the children were released for Christmas vacation, she did not invite her father to attend the ceremony.

"Don't you want Daddy to come?" a worried Amanda asked. Marianne, playing with her Gameboy, did not look up.

"He's too busy to come," she responded finally. "He has to build stuff and play racquetball with his friends."

Clearly, Marianne understood – or thought she understood – where she ranked in her father's world: just after making money and engaging in recreational pursuits. And, Amanda realized, the child was fearful of risking her heart again.

More serious was the effect George's neglect was having on their son. That fall, George had reluctantly promised to attend his son's championship football game. But when the day arrived, George flew to Florida to play golf with important investors. Peter had known the whole time that his father wasn't in the stands, and it affected his game. In the end, his team lost, and their coach had to break up a fight between Peter and two of his teammates, who blamed their loss on his bad performance.

Peter had been in a foul mood ever since. When his father came home from work, Peter immediately went into his room and shut the door. During dinner, Peter declined to speak to anyone, finishing his meal as quickly as he could so he could shut himself back in his room.

"It's just something kids go through," George had said irritably when Amanda brought up the matter of their son's unhappiness. "It's something they go through if their fathers don't make time for them," she had told him heatedly.

Slipping on her sapphire earrings, Amanda sighed. What had happened to the loving husband and father of just a few years ago? Why had money become so important to him? They already had more than they would ever spend.

Amanda stood up and surveyed herself in the mirror. Then, slipping on a fur coat, she left the apartment, closing the door softly behind her.

Chapter 4

At 9:15 p.m., George Bailey strode into the museum, crossed its pink marble-floored lobby, and headed for the public space where the ball was being held. He immediately sought out the bar.

"Double brandy," he said brusquely.

He glanced around the ballroom. The committee had decided on a Forties theme this year, and the band belted out songs from the war years: "I Got a Gal in Kalamazoo," "Too Marvelous for Words," and "I'll Be Seeing You." Servers dressed as bellhops and cigarette girls were deftly handing round appetizers. Signs reading "Buy your war bonds here," "Loose lips sink ships" and "Keep mum, she's not so dumb" covered the walls, along with enlarged photos of war heroes, FDR and Churchill, and film stars like Bette Davis, Joan Crawford, and John Wayne entertaining at the Hollywood canteen.

As he sipped his drink, George's eyes searched for Amanda. He finally located her across the ballroom, talking quietly to a friend. She was wearing her midnight blue silk evening gown, her blonde hair swept sleekly up, revealing the diamond and sapphire earrings George had given her on their 10th anniversary in Venice. She was, George thought, the most beautiful woman in the room, not just because of her slim figure and lovely face, but also because of the heart-stopping sweetness of her expression. What an asset she'd always been to his business, George thought, not for the first time.

He suddenly remembered the summer day they had met at a house party in the Hamptons. She'd caught his eye immediately. Her hair was gathered up into a sophisticated twist, and a sleek white dress showed off her lovely figure. He'd asked about her, and discovered she was the daughter of a wealthy diplomat. He'd half expected this rich and beautiful girl to be a bit on the sassy side. Instead, Amanda Burke was warmly vivacious, much like George's grandmother. She would not abandon the man who'd brought her to the party, but allowed George to take down her phone number.

He'd called her the next day and invited her to lunch with him at the Plaza. Amanda, he learned, had been born in Washington D.C., and grown up in embassies in Paris, London, and Madrid. She spoke French and Spanish fluently. She had studied art history at the Sorbonne and now worked at New York's Museum of Modern Art.

The couple wed eight months later and honeymooned in Florence. Amanda had continued working for MoMA until the birth of their son, Peter.

George determinedly pushed out of his mind thoughts of the noisy activists who'd shown up in front of his home that evening, and the bad publicity they were generating. Slipping through the dancing couples, George made his way to his wife. He touched her arm, and as she turned to him, smiled down at her.

"May I have this dance?" he asked.

She didn't smile back, but she allowed him to lead her onto the dance floor. The band swung into "Avalon."

Hoping to put Amanda in a better mood, George held her more closely and squeezed her hand.

"Remember?" he murmured. "They played this at our wedding."

"I remember," Amanda responded expressionlessly. George spun her into a turn, then pulled her close again. "Are you still angry at me about not going to Bedford Falls for Christmas?" he asked.

"No," she replied. "I'm not angry."

Puzzled and a little irritated, George said no more. When, he wondered in annoyance, had his wife become another problem to be solved? Amanda had never been one of those women who made you guess why she was upset with you, and she never sulked when she didn't get her way. But tonight she would not smile at him, would not even look at him, and she held herself stiffly against his embrace. Suddenly, the day's frustrations overwhelmed his desire to try to have a good time tonight.

"All right," he said brusquely. "Let's have it."

Amanda released herself from his arms and stepped back. George saw the color rise in her cheeks as she looked him in the eye for the first time that evening. "I'm not going to Vermont with you. I'm taking the children to spend Christmas in Bedford Falls with the family."

"Amanda," George began.

"I don't care about your friends at the city planning commission. I don't like them, and I've never even met their wives. You haven't seen your grandmother for two years, and she's not going to live forever. And" – she abruptly swung to a different subject – "you don't seem to realize how much the kids need you."

George pulled her back into his arms, spun her into another turn, and glanced about the dance floor to make sure nobody was overhearing them. Amanda's lips began to tremble, and tears shone in her eyes.

"Do you have any idea how little time you've spent with Marianne and Peter this past year? Or with me?"

George pressed his lips together tightly, knowing better than to interrupt.

"Let me tell you something, George. You're not the man I married. And don't give me that look," she added, her voice hardening. "You're obsessed with work, and with power, and status. All you care about is being seen at the right party, and getting your picture in the newspapers. Your idea of being a good husband is getting *my* picture in the papers.

"I'm not your wife anymore. I'm just another status symbol to you."

The orchestra launched into "String of Pearls." Across the ballroom, a woman laughed a bit too loudly. "The kids – our children, George" – Amanda swallowed hard – "Do you remember how you felt when Peter and Marianne were born? Do you? They were so precious to you. There was nothing you wouldn't have done for them. But now" – tears were running freely down her cheeks – "You barely remember they exist. Their lives just aren't important to you."

"That's not true."

"It *is* true. And they know it's true. Do you know how it feels for Peter to know you'd rather go to a party or a golf game than go to his football games? Do you know how Marianne feels at your lack of attention? She remembers when you sought her out the minute you got home to give her a hug. At least-" Amanda wiped her eyes with both hands. "At least the other dads have the sense to say they can't spend time with them because they have to work. But you don't even bother to hide your lack of interest in their lives. It breaks their hearts."

People were beginning to stare at them, George noticed. He took Amanda in his arms again, resuming the dance. His eyes searched for an exit. "I'm embarrassing you, aren't I?" Amanda said tightly.

"No, but I think you need to calm down."

"Please, George. I know that look. You can't wait to get me out of here."

"Can we just finish this dance?" George snapped irritably. "We can finish this conversation when we get home."

"It's already finished, George. And I'm beginning to think our marriage is, too."

"Oh, for heaven's sake, Amanda – "

"What do you think our marriage is? One of your big deals? You think if you just throw a little more money at me, or threaten me with lawyers, that you can fix this?"

"Amanda – "

Unconsciously, George tightened his grip on her arms. She jerked away from him.

"I'm going to Bedford Falls for Christmas with the kids. And I just might stay there when Christmas is over."

The song ended. The dancers applauded the musicians, who smilingly stood and bowed.

A stunned George watched as his wife walked to the cloakroom, retrieved her coat, and left the museum.

Saturday, December 15, 2007

Chapter 5

*S*nowflakes were falling softly on the streets and houses and lawns of Bedford Falls. They had been drifting down steadily for seven straight days. Wind had blown drifts nearly twenty inches high over mailboxes, bushes, and fences, and snowplows had kicked up dirty snow on the sidewalks, making it difficult to walk on them.

Zuzu Bailey Brown, standing at the window of her mother's house at 320 Sycamore, was glad to see the snowflakes drifting down despite the trouble they caused. Falling flakes were lovely, and they covered the grime of the little town, making it look almost the way it had when she was a little girl, growing up in the 1940s.

Zuzu sighed, and pushed back her shoulder-length, curly blonde hair. At sixty-seven, she was still slim and pretty, and her cheerfulness had always made Zuzu a favorite with the people of Bedford Falls. But now lines of sorrow creased her face as she reflected on the changes that had come to her home.

Bedford Falls, with its old, Victorian-style houses, small businesses, and friendly neighbors, had not changed much before her father died in 1989 – or if it had, the changes had been largely for the good. But since his death eighteen years ago, things had gone downhill fast.

First, a bar had opened on north Genesee Street – not like Martini's friendly gathering place, but one that served men as many drinks as they wanted, not caring if they drove home afterward and perhaps caused an accident.

During the Nineties, there began to be whispers that first one family man, and then another – men Zuzu knew from church – were drinking too much because of the stress of being out of work, and becoming alcoholics. Even worse, some of them had begun to take it out, violently, on their wives and children.

And then, when the antique shop down the street went out of business, another bar opened up in its place. Citizens had protested, but to no avail. It was too late, they were told; the bar's owner had had his business license approved.

And then came the video store that carried X-rated films. When a company that rented films by mail began taking away its business, the store closed, only to re-open as a men's club, complete with pole dancers. Quite a few out-of-towners came to visit the club. Sometimes, when they staggered out, drunk, they made offensive comments to passing women.

The people of Bedford Falls, alarmed at what was happening to their town, protested and picketed, but it didn't do any good. They went to City Hall, only to be told how much revenue the club was putting into the town coffers. One of them – a man who had not lived in Bedford Falls very long – told them that, after all, if they didn't like the club, they didn't have to patronize it.

And then a grocery store – part of a big, national chain – opened up just outside of Bedford Falls. A few years later, it had quietly installed a self-serve lottery vending machine. Soon it was also carrying pornographic magazines.

Family businesses that had been open for decades were now being forced to close, unable to compete with the low prices the big chain stores could offer. The families that ran the floral shop and the little bakery were among the first to close their doors; the big, new grocery store offered both an in-store bakery and cheaper flowers. The family-owned toy store followed; the big-box toy store that had opened up near the big new grocery store bought everything in bulk and sold them at much cheaper prices.

The more fortunate store owners, resigned to their fate, went to work for the chain stores; the less fortunate ones went bankrupt. When the economy went south, families that had lived in Bedford Falls for generations had little choice but to sell their homes and take jobs in other towns and cities. When they left, they took with them their memories of how small-town life ought to be lived.

A health clinic, so called, had opened up in the center of town. It passed out brochures to the town's teenagers, inviting them in for services that its staffers said their parents didn't need to know about. Between the encouragement to violate the teachings of church and family, and the carelessness typical of teenagers, the town's teen pregnancy rate shot up alarmingly. Outraged parents protested the clinic, only to be told patronizingly that teenagers had rights, too.

Even the things Zuzu's father had so lovingly built, or contributed money to, were beginning to deteriorate. The Bedford Falls Hospital, for instance, was looking a bit bedraggled. It needed so many things, including more incubators for premature babies, and a trauma center. The year before, when the Higgins child, pretending to be Spiderman, had jumped off his parents' roof, he'd been helicoptered to a nearby city for treatment for multiple broken bones and a concussion.

Bedford Falls ought to be able to provide its own trauma care, Zuzu thought, as she filled a vase with holly branches and placed it on the fireplace mantel. If only her father were still around, he'd have done something about it. Or someone like him – someone who had the same determination and ability to protect the town, and who was willing to sacrifice for it, if necessary.

Since retiring from Zuzu's Petals two years before, the widowed Zuzu had sold her home and moved in with her mother, now ninety-seven years old. A few weeks before, Mary Bailey had caught a cold that turned to pneumonia. Zuzu hired a nurse to care for Mary, while she herself made soups and read to her during the long winter afternoons. Two days ago, her sister Janie, who lived down the street, had come over to help her decorate Mary's Christmas tree and hang a wreath on the front door while Mary watched from the sofa, warmly wrapped in colorful knitted afghans.

While Mary was as cheerful as ever, her condition was not improving. Zuzu's greatest fear was losing her precious mother. Today, Mary had sipped the chicken bouillon Zuzu had brought her for lunch, taken her medicine, and then closed her eyes for a nap. Zuzu wondered if she was awake now. She walked quietly to her mother's bedroom door and put her ear up to it. She could hear her mother stirring.

Zuzu opened the door a crack. Mary was sitting up in bed, holding a cameo of her late husband taken when he was a young man. A little smile came over Mary's still-lovely face. She began to sing, very softly. Zuzu strained to hear.

"Buffalo gals can't you come out tonight, can't you come out tonight, can't you come out tonight, Buffalo gals can't you come out tonight and dance by the light of the moon...."

Chapter 6

At 9 a.m., George Bailey opened his eyes. He'd overslept, but then, he'd been up late the night before. He was meeting friends at 10 a.m. for racquetball at his sports club.

Stretching, he remembered Amanda's words at the dance. She was going to bail on their planned trip (okay, *his* planned trip) to Vermont and spend Christmas with the family in Bedford Falls. She'd threatened to stay there, but she'd been upset when she said it. Obviously, she and the children had to come back. The children were enrolled in expensive city schools, and Amanda had all her committees.

In the bathroom, George pulled off his pajamas and turned on the shower. Maybe, he reflected, turning his face into the spray, Amanda *should* take the kids to Bedford Falls. He could go to Vermont alone; it would do more harm than good if Amanda were in a bad mood in front of his friends on the city planning commission.

As for the rest of her complaints – that he wasn't a good father to Peter and Marianne – he'd find some way to smooth her down. Maybe he could take Peter to a Knicks game in January. He made a mental note to tell his personal assistant, a young lawyer named Ron Ayers, to get him some tickets. As for Marianne – he'd figure out something to do with her, too. Little girls were easy to please.

Over breakfast, he apologized to Amanda for their quarrel of last night. Of course it wasn't *his* fault, but wives always seemed to expect their husbands to apologize, anyway. She accepted his apology, but her face looked sad.

"You're right," he went on, "I'm not spending enough time with the kids. I'll take Peter to a Knicks game next month. He'll like that."

Amanda, sipping her coffee, nodded agreement. "Good," she said.

"I also think you're right to want to go to Bedford Falls for Christmas," he added, pouring himself a glass of orange juice. Amanda's face lit up.

"Oh, I'm so glad! Your grandmother will be so happy to see you. And she'll love seeing the kids again. They've grown – "

"No, wait. I meant that you and the kids should go. But I can't break my plans to go to Vermont with the De Lucas and the Kaufmans."

Amanda's face fell again. "You mean you want to spend Christmas apart? We've never done that before."

"Well – " George sighed, hoping Amanda wasn't building up for another explosion. "I just don't see any alternative. De Luca and Kaufman are important members of the city planning commission. I need them to go along with my plans to rezone that piece of property down by the river. I can't just – "

"Oh, never mind," Amanda snapped. "Do what you want. You always do, anyway."

Chapter 7

"Leticia," her mother said, "I told you to put your clothes and toys in those boxes."

Five-year-old Leticia, who'd spent her entire life in apartment 319 in the Trent Towers, stuck out her bottom lip. "I don't want to move!"

Her mother sighed. "I don't either, baby, but we don't have any choice. We have to be out of this apartment just after Christmas. You know that."

"But I don't want to move in with Aunt Tiana!" Leticia exploded. "I don't want to sleep in Kayla and Destiny's room. I want my own room!"

"And as soon as I can afford it, we'll move to our own place again," her mother answered as she stacked books into a box. "We're lucky Aunt Tiana will have us."

"Why do we have to move?" It was a question she'd asked over and over again, knowing the answer, but unable to accept it.

"Because Mr. Bailey, the man who owns this building now, wants to turn it into a place for rich folks to live."

"Why?"

"To make money, I guess. Now come on, Leticia, start packing up those toys."

Leticia's anger had no place to go but out. "I hate Mr. Bailey," she raged. "He's the meanest man in town!"

Chapter 8

George Bailey had just left his fitness club and was walking down Fifth Avenue, inhaling with pleasure the smells of New York: bagels from a tiny bakery, hot dogs from a food cart, and freshly roasted chestnuts. His cell phone rang. It was his personal assistant at Bailey Investments, Ron Ayers.

"Yes?" he answered brusquely.

"Got another call from the contractor on the McClure project," Ayers said. "He says he had to take out more load-bearing walls than he expected because the roof's been leaking for years, and most of the walls were rotten. He says we need to add some supporting beams to make up for it, which means he can't possibly finish the first penthouse apartment before Christmas, or that sixth floor apartment, either, especially with all the builders getting off for a few days of vacation. He suggests – "

George broke in. "I don't care what he suggests. We've promised two more families they could move in on December 21 so they could celebrate Christmas in their new homes. I don't care what he has to do, but those two apartments *must be finished* by then. Or else."

There was silence on Ayers' end as he fought to keep his temper. He knew the boss didn't like to be told that his plans and promises would have to be altered, but the contractor had been adamant. The apartments simply could not be finished until after the new year. George didn't give him a chance to respond.

"I chose this contractor because he has a reputation for bringing projects in on time," he began.

Sure, Ayers thought. *If you don't mind shoddy work.*

"But the rotten supporting walls means bringing the architect back in to determine the size and placement of the beams – " Ayers began. George cut him off.

"Tell him to have his men work round the clock, if necessary, but those apartments must be ready for occupancy by the twenty-first."

Ayers sighed. "Okay, boss, I'll tell him."

"You do that."

George hung up.

Sunday, December 16, 2007

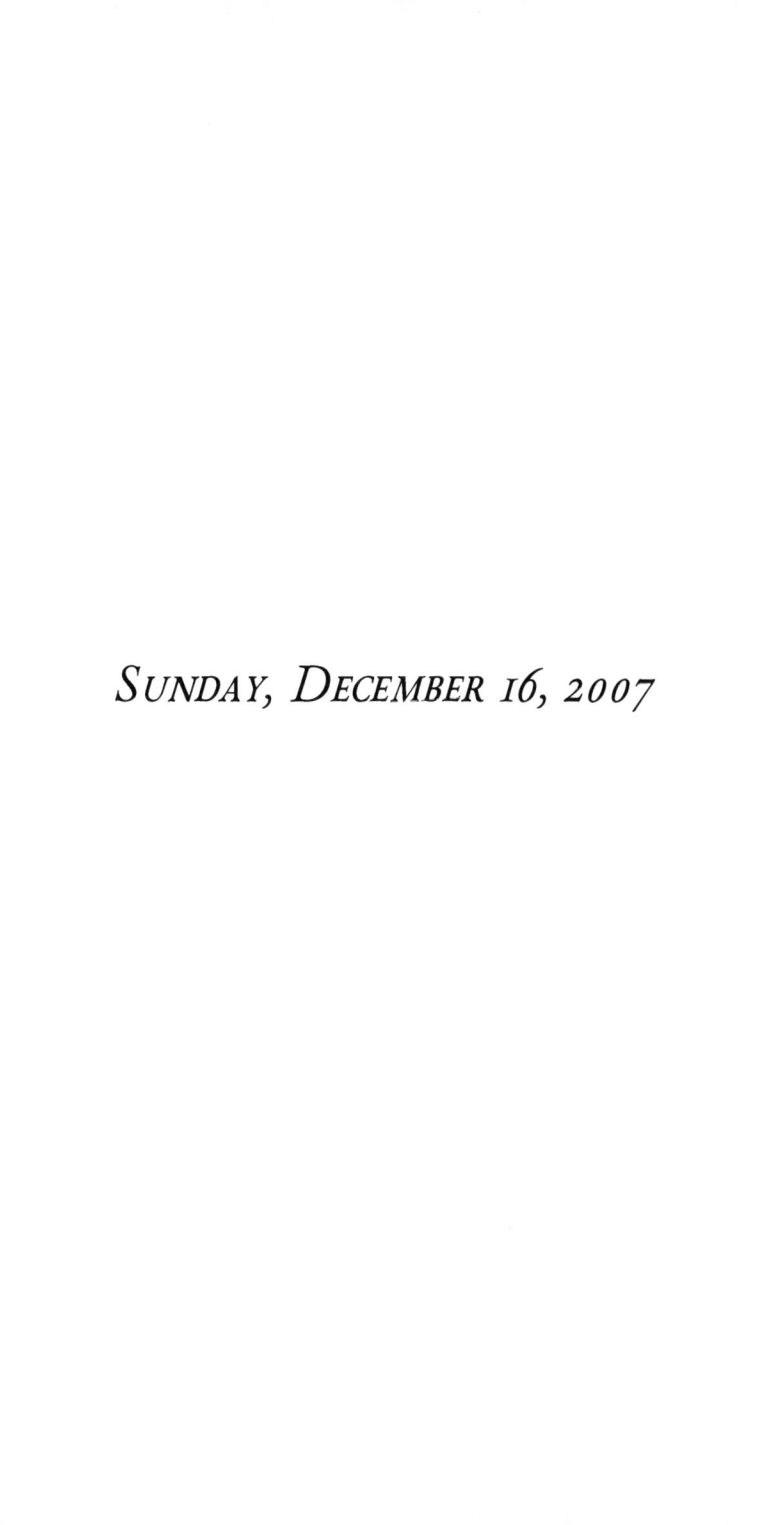

Chapter 9

At the Bedford Falls Presbyterian Church, Janie's and Zuzu's children and grandchildren lined the second pew from the front, the younger ones squirming and giggling. Short, dark-haired Janie was seated at the organ at the left of the altar, just in front of the white-robed choir. She was wearing the red wool dress she always wore through Advent, with the little Christmas tree brooch pinned to the front – the one her father had given her when she was sixteen.

Softly, Janie began playing the prelude.

Zuzu had personally arranged the flowers at the altar – an arrangement of red roses and white lilies – as she did every week. They looked beautiful, she thought.

Tommy Bailey sat near the back. He did not attend services often – he often had a hangover on Sunday morning – but when he did, Zuzu sat with her brother instead of her children and grandchildren, wanting Tommy to feel welcome.

White candles threw soft light over the altar, where a large crèche scene was carefully arranged on straw, still minus the baby Jesus and the Wise Men. Tall pine trees, swathed in white twinkle lights, rose majestically on either side of the altar, scenting the air with the smell of Christmas.

As latecomers found their seats, Janie began playing the first hymn of the third Sunday of Advent. The congregation rose to sing.

> *"While shepherds watched their flocks by night,*
> *all seated on the ground;*
> *the angel of the Lord came down*

*and glory shone around,
and glory shone around."*

When the congregation finished the final stanza, the Reverend Trevor Davis welcomed his flock. Zuzu liked him. The Davises had lived in Bedford Falls even longer than the Baileys had. Trevor's wife, Caroline, frequently visited Mary, and all three of the Davis boys were in the children's choir – probably not by choice, Zuzu thought with an inward grin, thinking of the athletic Davis sons.

The Grassley family stood up to light the advent candles. "This is the prophecy candle," little Brianna Grassley said, while her brother Samuel lit the first purple candle. "This is the Bethlehem candle, this is the shepherds' candle ..."

Watching the children, Janie could not help thinking about Brianna's great-grandmother, who had died some years ago: Violet Bick, who was known, in her younger years, as the loosest woman in town. While Janie's own mother had worked with the USO during the war while juggling four young children, Violet had been caught raising the morale of one sailor too many. She'd been asked to leave the USO, and many of the women of Bedford Falls began traveling to nearby Seneca Falls to have their hair done rather than patronize the beauty parlor owned by "that Violet Bick."

Ashamed and embarrassed, Violet had come to Janie's father on Christmas Eve of 1945 to close out her account so she could make a new start in New York City. Daddy had insisted on giving Violet a little extra money from his own pocket, and she'd gratefully kissed him goodbye, giving rise to nasty rumors that had reached the ears of Old Man Potter within hours.

In the end, Violet had changed her mind, deciding to stay in Bedford Falls and start over. She'd sold the beauty parlor and managed to get a job selling cosmetics at the old Emporium. She'd also started attending church – something her mother, an alcoholic, and her father, who'd abandoned the family when Violet was five years old, had never encouraged her to do. At first, the church ladies had been suspicious of Violet's change of heart. But they soon found her a willing volunteer.

One night, as Violet brought hot coffee and doughnuts to an Alcoholics Anonymous meeting in the church basement, she caught the eye of a middle-aged man. He was a former Marine named Frederic Spedden who was suffering from battle fatigue and struggling to break his reliance on gin. After a year-long courtship, Violet married Spedden, and the couple went on to have seven children.

All Violet had really needed, Janie thought, as she moved to the more comfortable padded chair near the organ, was the knowledge that she was truly loved. By the late 1980s, most of Violet and Frederic's children had moved away, but daughter Esther, now fifty-six, was still there, running Esther's Place, a home for unmarried teen mothers whose families had kicked them out. Her daughter, Louise Grassley, and her husband had brought their two children to Bedford Falls for the holidays. Another of Violet's granddaughters, Amy Blaine, would be arriving in a few days from Ohio, Janie had heard.

Brianna and Samuel Grassley seemed like nice children, Janie thought – although Brianna, with her blonde hair, blue eyes, and mischievous expression, looked exactly like Violet. Would history repeat itself? Janie wondered as she settled back to hear the sermon. She hoped not.

Chapter 10

"Another one, please, Larry."

Tommy Bailey was sitting at a stool in the Mongoose Bar at the north end of Genesee Street. A dusty plastic Christmas tree sat in the window, just below the big electric signs advertising the Schlitz and Budweiser brands. Holiday carols poured out of the cheap music system, competing with the sounds of a basketball game coming from the television set perched over the counter.

The smell of spilled beer floated up to Tommy, and he kicked aside the used napkins at his feet. Why did he always come to this crummy place? he wondered. The answer was that they served the cheapest drinks in town, and didn't cut him off, the way the Martinis did after just two drinks. And the Martinis were family!

Tommy sipped his drink, feeling sorry for himself. He thought of his father, now dead eighteen years, and of his sick mother, who was probably dying. His nieces and nephews, who had enjoyed Uncle Tommy's goofy jokes when they were small, now seemed to avoid him. Although they were polite, he knew they didn't respect him. As for his nephew George…

Anger rose in Tommy's chest. He remembered the way George had looked at him the last time he was in Bedford Falls two years ago, when Janie and Roberto had hosted the family for Thanksgiving dinner. He had not been able to disguise the look of contempt quickly enough when Tommy looked his way. Was it because he was so overweight – or because he was a failure?

Tommy could barely remember the hard times when he was a child.

His father had inherited Old Man Potter's money when Tommy was five years old. While his brother and sisters could remember drafty rooms, hand-me-down clothes, and cheap meals like tuna casserole and spaghetti, he had grown up in a house filled with warmth, nice clothes, new toys, and his father's favorite steak and mashed potatoes every week.

Not long after his father had died, Tommy had moved back into the family home "to take care of Mother," as he told Zuzu and Janie. He mowed the lawn, did some of the grocery shopping, and took out the garbage. Mary's housekeeper, Makina Mwangi, did the rest. When Zuzu moved in two years ago, she had begun cooking meals for both Tommy and Mary on Makina's days off.

Tommy finished his drink. Why couldn't he have been more like his siblings? He remembered the last time he'd seen Janie, when she'd come over to help Zuzu decorate their mother's Christmas tree. He'd seen the same look in her eyes as he occasionally saw in Zuzu's: pity. And once, by accident, a Bedford Falls old-timer had addressed him as "Uncle Billy" before quickly correcting himself.

Uncle Billy, Grandfather's loser brother. The guy who walked around with a bird on his shoulder and strings tied around his fingers.

"Another one, Larry," he said.

"Sure, Tommy. Coming right up."

Chapter 11

Brian Fulmer, construction manager for G. Saunders Construction, was working on a Sunday, something his wife didn't like him to do. But working weekends and nights was not going to get this job done when Mr. Bailey wanted it done. He watched as his men began pulling out the last of the walls from the seventh-floor apartment. Bailey Investments had decided to leave the apartments on the lower floors the same size, but wanted to turn the apartments on the top floor into airy lofts. But then they'd discovered that the walls holding up the ceiling were rotten, the victims of a roof that had been leaking for years.

Supporting beams needed to be added, but that would take weeks. They'd have to bring back the architect and the structural engineer, and then have lumber specially ordered and cut to fit the dimensions of this building. That would add to the cost of the project, as well as take up time they didn't have.

They'd managed to finish apartment 610 the day before. They'd put a rush on getting the appliances installed, and as soon as the new paint dried, the Bradshaw family could move in. But as for apartment 701...

Brian Fulmer thought hard. He knew he should be calling the structural engineer right now. But were the walls really that bad? He took another long look at them, thought about the bonus Bailey Investments had promised him for getting the project done on time, and made his decision.

"Hey, Kev," he called to one of his workmen.

"Yeah?"

"We're going to keep the old beams, after all. Go ahead and start painting the walls."

Kevin Drake stared at Brian. "But the walls – "

"Just do it," Brian responded, his expression hardening.

Kevin shrugged. "Okay. It's your funeral," he muttered under his breath.

Chapter 12

The front doorbell rang. Zuzu went to answer it.

"Hey there!"

It was Mary's next-door neighbor, Naomi Satinover. She held up a covered pot.

"Chicken soup with chive dumplings!"

"Oh, Naomi, I don't know where you find the time, between your kids and your law practice," Zuzu said. "Come on in."

"I wish I could, but I have to take the kids to have dinner with their grandparents in Rochester."

Zuzu took the pot.

"It smells fantastic!" she said, lifting the lid and taking a sniff.

"My mother's recipe. Guaranteed to cure whatever ails you. I hope Mary enjoys it." Naomi pushed a lock of her dark hair behind her ear.

"Is she doing any better?"

Zuzu's smile faltered. "No, not really."

Naomi gave her a sympathetic look. Both knew Mary could die soon; there was no need to pretend otherwise.

"Well – gotta run. Send the pot back over when you have time."

"Will do. And thanks again."

Chapter 13

After putting the soup into the refrigerator, Zuzu sat down at her computer, turned it on, and began an email to her nephew.

Dear George, she wrote. *Just wanted to touch base with you since we may not be seeing you this Christmas. Your grandmother is not recovering from the pneumonia – she's still weak and Dr. Baldwin comes to see her every day.*

Zuzu wondered if George would view this as pressure to come home to Bedford Falls for Christmas. When she'd last spoken to Amanda about it, George's wife had been unable to give her a definite answer.

We're so grateful to Dr. Baldwin – he doesn't charge for the daily visits because, he says, it was your grandfather who paid for his medical school education.

George – I wanted to bring up something before I had a chance to forget it. As you know, I'm on the board of the Bedford Falls Hospital. The hospital is in real need of some capital improvements, including a trauma center. Your grandfather spent most of the money he inherited or earned; what's left is going for the support of your grandmother or tied up for things like college scholarships.

If you can see your way to doing so, the hospital would greatly appreciate a donation from you and Amanda.

I hope we can talk about this more if you are able to come to Bedford Falls with the kids. Even if you are not able to make a donation at this time, I hope you know how much your grandmother, Aunt Janie, and the rest of the family would like to see you. With love,

Aunt Zuzu

She read the letter over and hit "send," sending up a prayer that George was in a generous mood when he read it.

Chapter 14

Agnes Hubbard stood in her apartment in the Trent Towers building, her home of sixty-four years. She had come here as a bride and reared her children here. She'd known everybody on her floor, and many of the residents of the other floors as well. She knew the owner of the grocery store a block away, the name of the young man who sold magazines and newspapers at a nearby stand, and the ladies who worked in the library, who greeted her by name when she came in to borrow books.

But her daughter had moved to Texas with her husband, her son was working in Saudi Arabia for an oil company, and her other son had died in Vietnam.

Agnes was almost the last resident left in the building. She had made no arrangements to move elsewhere. She didn't want to live anywhere else. And now she stood, looking around at all her dearest possessions – the photographs, the old mahogany furniture, the flower-patterned drapes she'd sewn and hung thirty years before.

Goodbye, she thought.

Agnes walked into her tiny kitchen and pulled open the door to the gas oven. She dragged a dining room chair over to the oven, closed the door to the hall, and stuffed dish towels beneath it.

And then she dropped tiredly onto the chair and turned on the gas.

Monday, December 17, 2007

Chapter 15

"How many people are still living in Trent Towers?" George was pacing his glass-walled office at Bailey Investments.

Ron Ayers, seated on a sofa covered in beige raw silk, checked his notebook. "People are still living in three of the units. All the rest have left," he answered.

"Send them another reminder – no, a warning – that they have to be out by December 31," George ordered.

"Will do," Ayers replied. *And after the New Year, I'm looking for another job. One where my boss can provide documentary evidence that he's an actual human being.*

Ron turned to leave, and found Amanda Bailey standing in the outer office.

"Hello, Mrs. Bailey," he said warmly. He liked George's wife. So did everyone else at Bailey Investments. Amanda smiled back at him.

"Hello Ron. How are you?"

"I'm good. Here to see Mr. Bailey?"

"Yes, if he's not too busy."

"I don't think he's doing anything at the moment."

Amanda knocked softly on her husband's door. He glanced up and immediately looked wary.

"Hi," he said. "Come on in."

Amanda entered and sat down at a chair before George's desk. Gazing up at him, she felt more like a client than his wife.

On Sunday they had scarcely spoken to one another. George had spent much of the day in his study with the door closed, working and watching a ball game. "I thought," she said tentatively, "that we could try to resolve this thing with Christmas."

George sighed inwardly. Not this again.

"Maybe," Amanda said carefully, watching his face, "you could spend Christmas Eve and Christmas Day in Bedford Falls, and then go to Vermont."

George appeared to consider her suggestion. There was another week to go before Christmas Eve; he didn't want to spend it arguing with his wife. He had too much to focus on at work just now. If he could just dangle a little hope in front of her ...

"That might work," he said. "Let me think about it."

Amanda's face brightened. "Thanks."

"I'll be home around seven," he said, as Amanda rose to leave.

The door to George's office was abruptly pushed open. It was Ron Ayers, his face white.

"Boss, turn on CNN," he said.

Chapter 16

Seventeen-year-old Matthew Bailey Gruszecki, grandson of Zuzu Bailey, whistled as he zipped his jacket and pulled a ski cap over his light brown hair. He stepped out into the cold. It was still snowing, and the drifts were deeper than ever. Putting his gloved hands into his pockets, the tall, slender high school senior began the short walk to great-grandmother Mary's house.

Matt adored his great-grandmother. His great-grandfather had died before he was born, but he loved to hear stories about him from Mary, and from Grandma Zuzu.

The walk was a short one. He climbed the steps to his grandmother's house and knocked gently before letting himself in.

Zuzu was in the kitchen, washing up. "Hello, darling," she greeted him.

"How's Grandma Mary today?" he asked.

"About the same," Zuzu replied.

"Is she awake?"

"Yes, she is. I'm sure she'd love a visit from you. Why don't you go on in."

Mary's bedroom had been moved downstairs when she'd suffered a small stroke ten years before. Matt walked to her door and opened it a few inches.

"May I come in, Grandma Mary?" he asked.

Mary looked up and smiled. "Of course you may. It's good to see you."

Matt seated himself on the chair next to the bed. He noticed that

Mary was holding a small, framed picture of herself and Great-grandfather George on their wedding day, standing in front of the church in the rain while friends threw rice over them.

"You thinking about Great-grandpa?" he asked.

"Yes." The smile faded from Mary's face. "I can't help wondering what he would think about the way Bedford Falls has changed. And I know he'd be worried about your Uncle George."

"Is Uncle George in trouble?"

"No, but I don't think he's happy. I see him on the news now and then. He doesn't seem to be very well liked in New York. And I'm not sure he's..."

Tears slowly filled Mary's eyes as she thought of her grandson. *Entirely ethical*, was what she'd been about to say. What had happened, she wondered, to make money so important to George?

Matt hastily changed the subject to one he knew Grandmother enjoyed talking about. He reached out and took her hand.

"Tell me about what Bedford Falls was like when you were a girl," he prompted.

Mary's smile returned. Her eyes drifted away from his face as she began turning back the years in her mind.

"I grew up with your great-grandfather, you know," she began. "We lived just a few streets away from each other. After school, he worked at Gower Drugs, running errands and serving ice cream and candy to the rest of us."

"And he thought you were the prettiest girl in town, right?" Matt prompted.

"He didn't know I was alive." Mary smiled in amusement. "It was quite a few more years before he actually noticed me."

"At the high school dance in 1928."

"That's right. We had a good time that night, but then his father died of a stroke. He spent the summer clearing up his father's accounts. He was planning to go to college that September, but – "

"He decided to stay and run the Building and Loan."

"Yes. He felt he had to. He wasn't very happy about that. He wanted so badly to get an education. I went off to college in New York, and didn't see him again until the following summer. We ran into each other at parties and church and events around town, but things didn't really get rolling between us for another three years. We finally got married in 1932, and moved into this house when it was pretty run-down."

Mary was beginning to look sleepy. "Tell me about the people who lived here in those days," Matt urged quietly.

Mary's eyes opened wide. "Oh, they were wonderful people! Old Mr. Martini and his wife, and the Bishops, Uncle Billy and the cousins, my brother Marty, Bert O'Brien, the only policeman in the whole town, and old Mr. Gower, and Nick, the bartender at Martini's Place, and the Randalls, and Dr. Campbell, and the Kennedys and the Macklins and the Thompsons... They're all gone now – at least, the ones I knew. The ones I grew up with and who lived near us and went to church with us, and whose kids babysat my children when they were small."

Mary's lips trembled. "And your great-grandfather, of course. How I miss him! The town hasn't been the same since he died."

"What do you mean?" Matt asked.

Mary sighed, her hands smoothing the blanket that covered her. "You're too young to remember what Bedford Falls was like in the old days. Everybody knew everyone else. People cared about each other, and about the town – your great-grandfather most of all, although he didn't realize it for a long time. During the war, we all pulled together. And when Uncle Billy lost all that money – "

"Eight thousand dollars," Matt supplied. He knew the story well. Grandma Zuzu told it to him every Christmas.

" – the whole town contributed enough money to make it up. We didn't need to borrow a penny from Sam Wainwright – "

"Your old lover boy," Matt supplied again.

"Matthew!"

"Well, he was, wasn't he? Until Great-grandpa came along and stole you right out from under his nose."

"Nonsense. I didn't love Sam. I never loved anyone except George."

"Whatever happened to Sam Wainright?"

"Oh," Mary smiled wistfully. "He got very rich, and then he lost a lot of money, and then made more money. He divorced his wife and married again, and then divorced her and married someone else."

Mary's smile faded. "He stopped coming back to Bedford Falls. And then he died about thirty years ago when he was traveling through Europe. He wasn't that old, but I don't think he was very happy. And he didn't take very good care of himself."

"Did he have any kids?"

"He had one son who didn't turn out very well. I don't think Sam spent much time with him. The boy drank a lot, and went to parties, and drove fast cars. And then he drank too much one night and smashed his car up just outside New York City. He didn't survive."

Elsewhere in the house, Matt heard the sound of vacuuming. Makina was busily cleaning the upstairs rooms for the out-of-town relatives who would occupy them in a few days. Mary smoothed her hand over her blanket again. The diamond engagement ring George had given her in 1932 gleamed.

"Those years with Grandpa must have been wonderful years," Matt commented, hoping to get her mind off Sam Wainwright and his sad life.

Mary looked him straight in the eye. "Yes, they were good years. But they were *hard* years. Don't forget, darling, we started our married life during the Great Depression. And George didn't make much money. Why, I never even had a vacuum cleaner or a washing machine or dryer until we'd been married ten years. And I had to take care of four children. Sometimes I got so tired of being poor and having to work so hard. But then I reminded myself that I had won what I wanted most.

"Great-grandfather."

"That's right." Mary smiled, and looked down again at the wedding picture. She was silent for a minute, then asked Matt:

"Do you think the town would do that again?"

"Do what?"

"Donate a lot of money to someone in trouble."

Matt thought a moment. "It would depend on who was doing the asking," he finally said. He took out his iPhone and punched in some numbers. "Eight thousand dollars would be... just over ninety-two thousand dollars today."

"Good heavens!" Mary said. "I can't imagine the town being that generous."

Matt looked down at her. "I don't know, Grandma Mary. Some pretty nice people have moved here over the years. I like them. I think they'd help out in a crisis."

"I doubt it," Mary said sleepily. "I'd better take a nap now."

She reached out to pat his hand. "Thank you for visiting, Matthew. Tell your mother I said hello."

Chapter 17

"What's going on?" George Bailey asked as he reached for the controls and switched on CNN. The blonde talking head was standing in front of Trent Towers.

"Eighty-seven year old Agnes Hubbard was found dead this morning, an apparent suicide. She was among the last holdouts at the Trent Towers apartment building. Bailey Investments, the new owner of the building, had told residents they had to find somewhere else to live by December 31.

"But Agnes Hubbard had nowhere else to go," the blonde went on.

Of course she had somewhere else to go, George thought, his temper rising. *There are plenty of places for people to go if they don't have money.*

The blonde continued.

"Mrs. Hubbard had lived in her apartment for most of her life – sixty-four years, according to one of her neighbors."

The face of an older man now filled the screen.

"Mrs. Hubbard has been buying groceries from my store since 1943, when my father was running the place," he announced. "I know she was upset at having to leave. She didn't have no family nearby. I guess she just couldn't take the stress of having to get out."

The blonde came back, looking somber.

"Again, eighty-seven-year-old Agnes Hubbard was found dead this morning in her apartment in Trent Towers, where residents were ordered to leave by December 31. Bailey Investments plans to build luxury apartments in the space, with retail shopping and restaurants on the ground floor."

The expression on the blonde's face made it clear what she thought of Bailey Investments and its plans, George thought. But just in case viewers didn't get the picture...

"Like Mrs. Hubbard, many of those residents had nowhere to go. Some are in homeless shelters, and, CNN has learned, a few of them are now living on the streets. For CNN, I'm – "

George furiously clicked the television off, cursing under his breath. He'd forgotten that Amanda was there until he turned and saw her shocked face.

"You threw those poor people out onto the streets?" she whispered. Ron quietly left George's office, pulling the door shut behind him.

"Amanda, those people had plenty of notice," George began.

Amanda was staring at him as if she didn't know him.

"But that reporter said some of those people are living on the streets! How could you have done such a thing? You could have – you could have – "

"Amanda, let's talk about this at home," George interrupted, hoping to head off another quarrel.

"You could have let the old ones stay until they died." Amanda began to button her coat.

Agnes Hubbard did *stay until she died*, George thought viciously. "It's not my fault she committed suicide," he retorted. "Lots of people kill themselves every day. And if I'd let her and the others keep living there, maybe for years, we wouldn't have made any money on those apartments – "

"So what? George, we already have more money that we know what to do with. When are you going to finally have enough?"

Amanda picked up her handbag. She was still staring at him, an expression of disbelief on her face.

"What would your grandfather think if he saw you now?" she asked.

Turning, she left his office.

Tuesday, December 18, 2007

Chapter 18

"Aunt Zuzu?"

"Amanda!" Zuzu, picking up the kitchen wall phone, was delighted to hear from her nephew's wife. "How's everyone doing?"

Couldn't be worse. "We're fine."

Amanda had arrived home the previous afternoon, still shaking with shock over Agnes Hubbard's tragic death and George's indifference to it. She had prepared dinner for Peter and Marianne, then sent them to do their homework. She then sat in the glass-walled living room, gazing out at the lights of New York. Suddenly, she had felt swamped with a sense of loneliness.

Today, after getting the children off to school, Amanda had impulsively picked up the phone and called George's aunt. After exchanging pleasantries, Amanda took the plunge.

"I just wanted to let you know we'll be coming to Bedford Falls to spend Christmas with you and Mary and the rest of the family. George thinks he might be able to get away for a couple of days, at least. I'm sorry we waited so long before letting you know our plans."

"Oh, darling, that's wonderful news! Mother will be delighted to see you and the children again."

"How is Mary? Is she over her pneumonia?"

Zuzu's smile faded. "No, she's not much better. Dr. Baldwin stops in nearly every day to check on her, and we have a nurse looking after her, but, no, she's not really recovering the way she should."

"I'm sorry to hear that."

Zuzu knew Amanda meant it. Mary and Amanda had a special relationship. Few people called as often as Amanda did to check on Mary, and she frequently sent her small gifts from New York shops.

"When do you think you'll be here? If you come on the twenty-first, you'll be here in time for the Christmas parade on Saturday. And there's a square dance at the community center on the twenty-ninth, if you're up for that."

Amanda paused. While George might be talked into spending a day or two in Bedford Falls, she knew he would never agree to spending five or six days away from his business – unless it was time spent with business associates. Perhaps, she thought, she and the children could come early, and George could join them on Christmas Eve.

"That sounds great," she finally responded. We'll drive up on the twentieth, then."

"Oh, darling, I can't wait!" Zuzu enthused. "I'll have Makina get your rooms ready."

Chapter 19

Brian Fulmer dropped into a seat at a sports bar on 10th Street in the East Village and ordered a beer. His eyes wandered over the place, searching for the man he'd arranged to meet there that evening. He lit a cigarette and waited.

Ten minutes later, a rush of cold air blew in as someone opened the door.

It was him.

The man ordered his own drink and slid into the other side of the booth. The two men eyed one another. There was no need to make conversation. They had done this deal before, when Brian had needed this man to ignore violations of the city code on other buildings he'd had to finish on a tight deadline.

"Got the money?" the second man asked in a low voice.

Brian looked around, then pushed a thick envelope across the table.

Chapter 20

*T*welve-year-old Peter Bailey glanced down as his phone vibrated. It was a text from his friend Brad.

Lets go see Xmas Nitemare midnight Roxy. Bring bz.

Peter considered it. He would have to sneak out of the apartment, of course. His mother would never allow him to go to a film so late at night, especially an R-rated one. As for his father – a familiar bitterness pressed against his heart. His father didn't care what he did, as long as it didn't interfere with his work at Bailey stinking Investments.

Ok, he texted back. *C U there.*

Chapter 21

"I'm going to run to the market for a few things," Janie told her husband as she slipped into her down-filled overcoat and pulled on her gloves. Roberto Martini had taken a rare evening off, leaving his sons and nephews to run Martini's Place.

"I don't like you going out alone after dark," Roberto told her, running his fingers through his white hair.

"I need to get something for dinner, and I want to pick up the ingredients to make cookies for the grandchildren."

"Can't you go tomorrow morning instead?"

"No, tomorrow morning we have a rehearsal for the children's Christmas program. And then I want to visit Mother. Besides, it's only six o'clock, honey."

Roberto sighed. "Okay, wrap up warm."

Janie drove to the little Mom and Pop market in downtown Bedford Falls, which she preferred over the big superstore just outside town. She knew the names of everybody who worked there, and they knew hers. Thanks to the loyalty of longtime customers like Janie, the store had managed to stay open.

Janie grabbed a basket and gathered butter, eggs, nutmeg, flaked coconut, and chocolate chips, most of which were going into the Nanimo Bars she planned to make. She added pork chops, a head of lettuce, cucumbers, and cherry tomatoes.

"Hi, Carla," Janie greeted the checker. "How's your little boy?"

Carla Tucker scanned Janie's groceries and bagged them. "He's almost over his cold. Douglas is staying with him this evening."

"I'm glad he's better," Janie said. "We sure need his voice in the Christmas program."

Janie paid for her groceries and left the store, heading across Genesee Street to where she'd parked her car on Washington. Music and raucous laughter floated from Richard's Club for Men on the corner. Janie was waiting for the light to turn so she could cross the street when someone grabbed her arm and yanked her around.

It was a pair of drunks.

"How about a dance, schweetie?" the one holding her arm slurred. "Hey, Ted," he said to his companion. "This lady wanths to dance."

Ted laughed and nearly fell over. "She's too old to dance, Al. She has all her clothes on."

Janie yanked her arm away. Without a word, she stepped into the street. Al grabbed her again, this time around the waist. Losing his balance, he fell heavily against Janie, causing her to fall. She dropped her grocery bag to catch herself, but struck her right knee hard on the pavement.

Janie angrily struggled to get free of Al, who had fallen on top of her.

"Get off me!" she shouted furiously.

"Hey!" someone shouted from across the street.

A relieved Janie recognized the voice of her son Nicky. He and his brother Ed had just emerged from Martini's Place. They crossed the street in a few swift strides and helped their mother to her feet.

"You okay, Mom?" Nicky asked anxiously as he brushed the snow off her coat.

"I'm fine, honey," Janie responded, although her right knee throbbed from the impact of the fall.

The drunken Al still lay face down on the street. Ed looked at him with disgust. "This guy fall on you, Mom?"

"He wanted to dance with me," Janie replied, trying to laugh.

Ed muttered something in Italian.

"What was that?" Janie asked.

"I said, I hope a car runs over the stupid... so-and-so," Ed replied, glaring down at the man.

Al's friend Ted was now in the street, struggling to get his friend to his feet. He got him halfway up, and then dropped him. Al promptly vomited into the gutter.

"Come in and sit down for a minute, Mom," Nicky urged her.

"All right," Janie replied. "But not too long. Your father will get worried."

The three of them entered Martini's Place. Janie welcomed the warm, toasty atmosphere, the soft, jazzy music, and the white damask tablecloths. Roberto's nephew waved a welcome as he served customers.

The restaurant had been revamped several times over the years. Martini's Place had been little more than a bar when Roberto's late father, Giuseppe, had run it; now it had a fresh, contemporary flair, but still managed to maintain the friendly atmosphere it had exuded when Giuseppe Martini had run it with his friend Nick.

Nicky and Ed had quietly told their cousins what had happened to Janie. All of them were glowering. Janie reflected, not for the first time, that she had married into a very intense family. Nicky, Ed, and their cousins all wanted to go after the drunks and give them a piece of their minds, along with the impression of their boots on their backsides.

But then Janie remembered that Christmas of 1945, when her father had kicked over his painstakingly constructed model bridge. Get anyone upset enough, she thought, and they just might explode.

But her father had done this just once in his life, as far as Janie knew. The trouble with Bedford Falls was, too many people seemed to be exploding far too often. And too many people were getting hurt. Janie recalled the last time she had seen her friend Renee Randall, when Janie had stopped by her house with a cake for her birthday. Renee had opened the door and thanked Janie for the cake, but had not invited her in. Janie had been shocked to see the remains of a black eye marring Renee's pretty face. She knew Renee's husband had lost his job, but he had no business taking it out on his wife.

Janie and Renee attended the same church. Janie had wondered if she should mention the black eye to their pastor, whom she knew took a dim view of men who hit their wives and insisted that battered wives and their husbands live apart until the problem could be resolved. IF it could be resolved.

Janie sighed. What was happening to Bedford Falls? What was the answer to the town's growing problems?

Chapter 22

Peter Bailey's cell phone buzzed him awake at 11:30 p.m. He lay there listening for any sounds in the duplex. Everything was silent. Both his parents must have gone to bed, as they usually did, around 11.

Peter rose, put on his jeans, a shirt, a sweatshirt, and his boots. Zipping himself into his jacket, he tiptoed his way to his father's liquor cabinet. Opening the glass door, he pulled out a bottle of Scotch. He stuffed it into his backpack, walked to the front door, and stepped out. He went down the stairs instead of the elevator, and let himself out a back door in order to avoid questions from the doorman. Moments later, he was running down the dark street.

Wednesday, December 19, 2007

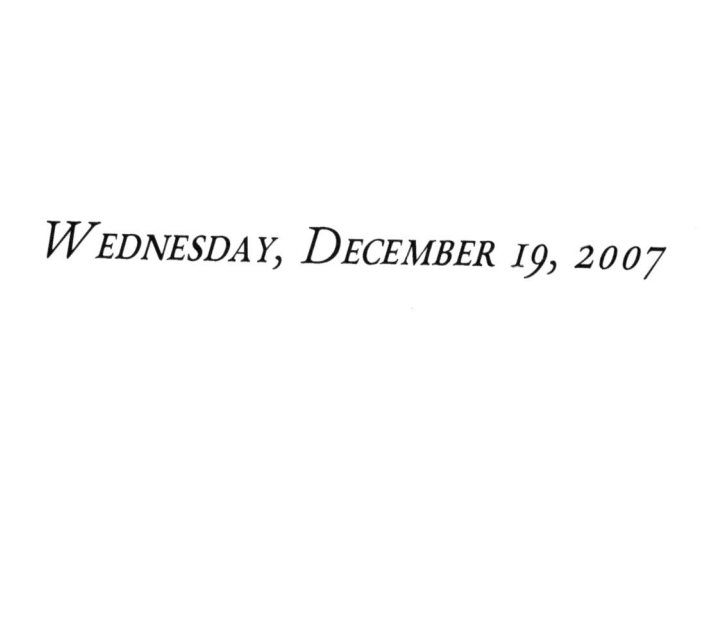

Chapter 23

Amanda's phone rang at 2:30 a.m. The number was unfamiliar. *Mary*, she thought. *She must be in the hospital.*

"Mrs. Bailey?"

"Yes."

"This is Sargent McGrath of the NYPD First Precinct."

Amanda was confused. Why would the police be calling her in the middle of the night?

"We have your son Peter Bailey here. We caught him and his friend breaking the windows of a building under construction. We'd like you to come pick him up."

"That's impossible," Amanda exclaimed, no longer bothering to keep her voice down. "He's at home in bed."

Beside her, George stirred.

Sargent McGrath had heard these words from parents many times.

"Ma'am, he has photo identification from his school. He's Peter Bailey, all right. Check your son's bed if you don't believe me. And then come down here and get him."

Chapter 24

George and Amanda huddled together in police station chairs, waiting to see their son. Thank God, he was all right, Amanda thought. Security guards had caught the boys throwing rocks through the windows of an unoccupied building a few blocks from their home, and called the police. Searching Peter's backpack, officers had found the half-empty bottle of Scotch.

What was taking so long? Amanda wondered, pushing a strand of blonde hair behind her ear. And then she saw her son coming through a door, Sargent McGrath behind him.

"We'll see you in court tomorrow afternoon," McGrath told them.

Amanda stepped forward and hugged her son. Her nose wrinkled as she recognized the sour smell of vomit. George, his face tight with anger, did not touch his son. Amanda knew he was thinking of the headlines if this incident became known. Journalists seem to take particular pleasure in exposing the misdeeds of the children of the rich.

"Let's go," George said curtly. "Wait – give me that bottle of Scotch first."

Peter silently unzipped his backpack and handed the bottle to his father.

George said nothing as he drove them back home. But once they were back in their apartment, and their downstairs neighbor, who'd come up to stay with Marianne, had gone home, he turned angrily to Peter.

"What possessed you to go out in the middle of the night and start throwing rocks through windows?"

Peter, unzipping his vomit-encrusted coat, did not reply.

"Answer me!" George shouted.

"We didn't go out to throw rocks! We went to see a movie," Peter replied sullenly.

"What movie? Which theater?" Amanda asked.

"What difference does it make what movie he saw?" George shouted. "Whose idea was it to steal my Scotch?"

"Mine."

He'd answered a trifle too quickly, and both his parents noticed.

"You are not to see Brad Lyons ever again," George growled.

"He goes to my school. I see him every day."

"Don't you dare talk back to me!" George shouted.

All three of them heard the sounds of muffled crying coming from Marianne's bedroom. Amanda stood up.

"That's enough for tonight, George," she said firmly. "We can talk about this in the morning. Peter, go back to bed."

Peter went to his room and shut the door. Amanda went to comfort Marianne. George made himself a drink and downed it swiftly. What was happening to his family?

He sank down into a wing chair and looked out at the lights of the city. He loved this glass-walled apartment with its phenomenal views, although Amanda had always thought the apartment – and much of the sculpture and paintings George had filled it with – too sterile. He loved New York, he loved his job as head of Bailey Investments, he loved his social life, and he loved his wife and kids. So why was everything suddenly going wrong?

Unexpectedly, thoughts of his grandfather, and of Bedford Falls, floated to the surface of his mind. He'd been born in Bedford Falls, and his parents had frequently dropped him off with his grandparents when they were traveling until he'd grown old enough to accompany them. His earliest memory was of his grandfather pulling him along in a little cart, past a white picket fence, past the pink Grandiflora hydrangea bushes in full bloom, filling his nose with their delicious scent, past his grandmother's black dachshund, Toots, panting in the July heat.

And then an abrupt left turn into the driveway of the big blue-painted house on Sycamore Street, where the smell of his grandmother's peach pie drifted out. He remembered the feel of his grandfather lifting him out of his cart, carrying him up the steps and setting him gently down on the white-painted porch. A screen door slamming, and his mother coming out to kiss his cheek before collapsing into a faded, chintz-covered chair and sipping her lemonade.

Later came the stories told at his grandfather's knee, along with books and songs and poetry. The two fished together in Mt. Bedford's mountain streams and hiked together in the woods. When he was two, Grandfather began taking him to Gower Drugs for ice cream. When he was five, Grandfather took him into the Savings and Loan and helped him open an account. When he was ten, and traveling with his parents, Grandfather had sent him a subscription to *National Geographic*. Hundreds of back issues of the magazine lived dusty lives on the shelves of Grandfather's library, George remembered.

Every Christmas Eve, after helping Grandfather decorate the tree with lights and angel ornaments, George lay on his back under the tree in his pajamas and robe, trying to guess what was in the wrapped boxes with his name on them, and waiting eagerly for his grandfather to tell his Christmas story once again. Outside, the snowflakes tumbling down in the darkness turned the old house into a Christmas card. Inside, a fire in the huge fireplace warmed the family, and Grandmother passed around a plate of walnut fudge.

George usually fell asleep as Aunt Janie played Christmas carols on the old piano, while her mother and father, brothers and sister, children, nephews, and nieces sang along. George knew his father carried him up to bed in his strong arms, because he always awoke there on Christmas morning, carefully tucked in.

After the sudden death of his parents when he was fourteen, George had been too numb with grief to truly appreciate the town or its people during the four years he'd lived with his grandparents. He knew, though, that his grandfather had been the most beloved figure in Bedford Falls, and that he's used most of the money he'd inherited on improvements to the town he'd spent more than twenty years trying to escape from.

George now wondered why it had never seemed to occur to his grandfather to invest the money instead, and double it, or even triple it. Instead, he'd seemed satisfied to live pretty much the way he always had, although he'd made dramatic improvements to the old house. It still had a late Forties look to it, as his grandparents had never seen any need to update the house one they had it the way they liked it.

His grandfather had been one of the happiest people he'd ever known. On that long-ago Christmas Eve in 1945, Grandfather's brother Harry had toasted him, calling him the richest man in town.

As George sat in his glass-walled penthouse duplex, decorated by one of the most famous design teams in the world, a small voice in his head asked him, *Are you happy, George Bailey?*

Was he?

Sighing, George picked up the paperwork the police had given him detailing why they'd picked up Peter. He glanced through it, and suddenly his eye was caught by the address of the building Peter and Brad had thrown rocks at.

It was the McClure building.

Thursday, December 20, 2007

Chapter 25

Janie Bailey Martini held open the door to the Tip Top Cafe for her daughter Gabriela and sixteen-year-old granddaughter Olivia, who was greatly enjoying her Christmas vacation. Inside the cheerful shop, filled with the smells of cappuccino, muffins, and damp clothing, Janie searched for her cousin Mavis. Mavis, the daughter of Mary Bailey's brother, Marty Hatch, had been born on the same day as Janie. The two seventy-one-year-olds had grown up just a few streets apart, and been best friends since toddlerhood.

The Tip Top Cafe had changed hands several times since it opened in 1921, but its rather cheerful name remained the same, even as the décor and food had altered.

Janie spotted Mavis, who waved and smiled from a table in a back corner. After ordering their coffee and pastries, Janie, Gabriela, and Olivia joined Mavis.

"Guess what!" Janie said, smiling. "George and Amanda and the kids are coming for Christmas!"

"Oh, that's great," Mavis exclaimed. "I suppose Amanda called Mary, and Mary told Zuzu, and – "

" – and Zuzu told you," Gabriela finished.

"And by tonight, the whole town will know," Olivia said with a grin. She twisted one of her long, brown braids in one hand as she sipped her latte with the other hand. "It'll be fun to see Peter and Marianne again, but I suppose Uncle George will be a grump, as usual." She made a face.

Gabriela looked across at her daughter tolerantly. Livvy, she considered, was old enough to say what she thought without having her mother harping on her that it wasn't nice "to say things like that." It was one of the reasons the two got along so well.

"I'm a little surprised he's coming," Gabriela acknowledged. "George has never really liked coming to Bedford Falls, even though most of the family lives here. And the West Coast relatives are coming this year, too."

Gabriela thought with pleasure of the fun they would have when the other branch of the Bailey family – Harry Bailey's descendants – arrived. Several of the younger ones worked for Google or Microsoft; one of them, Donald, worked at NASA and lived in Northern Virginia.

"I'm surprised Amanda talked him into it," put in Mavis.

The other women nodded in agreement as they nibbled their muffins and biscotti.

"I guess that means we'd better buy some gifts for them," Janie added. The family had a rule that no gifts were to be exchanged with relatives who lived too far away to celebrate Christmas together; doing so simply added unnecessary stress to the holidays. But now that George's family was coming to Bedford Falls...

"What do you get for the family that has everything?" Olivia asked, only half in jest.

"Good question," Gabriela replied. "We can get some board games for the kids – there's always something new coming out. But getting something for Amanda and George will be a little harder."

Janie thought for a few moments. "I could give Amanda a copy of my new Christmas CD," she said finally. "She'll like the music, and she'll love knowing that sales benefit the church restoration fund."

"And for George?" Mavis asked.

All four women thought hard. But nobody could think of anything to give a man as rich as George was.

"How about a book about how to achieve happiness by giving away your money?" Olivia asked mischievously.

The women laughed, and then fell silent. Young Olivia had hit on a painful truth, Janie thought. It had been two years since she'd seen George, but when he'd come to Bedford Falls for Thanksgiving in 2005, he did seem to be unhappy – unhappier than any man with his wealth had any right to be. And, she thought, he did far too little to help the less fortunate. Zuzu had told Janie about the brief email George had sent her in response to her plea for money for the hospital. Janie did not consider the opera society and art museums George supported as being among the "less fortunate."

"It's funny," Olivia mused, tearing a chunk off her blueberry muffin.

"What's funny?" her mother prompted.

"It's funny that Uncle George is Great-Grandfather George's grandson. Great-grandfather even wrote a little book about how happy he was when he had practically nothing. He was just so glad to have his wife and kids, and a place to live, and a job that allowed him to help other people."

"It took Daddy a long time to appreciate those things," Janie reminded her. "And he said it took an angel to help him do it."

The three older women exchanged glances and smiled. Seeing the glances and correctly interpreting them, Olivia asked, "Do you think Great-Grandfather really did see an angel?"

Janie smiled at her granddaughter. "Well, he said he did."

"You're avoiding the question!"

Janie laughed. "What are you, a prosecutor?"

"Not yet. Anyway, I'd really like to know what you think. Do you believe in angels? Do you think they come to earth to help us when we need it?"

Janie looked into her granddaughter's bright green eyes. "There's no reason, theologically, why they couldn't," she responded finally. "The Bible is full of accounts of angels coming down to help people, or advise them, or give them good news, the way Gabriel did with Mary."

"I know," Olivia said. "And I remember that one of the angels got kind of snarky with the father of John the Baptist, just because he couldn't believe his really, really old wife was going to have a baby. I mean, come on! Anybody would have trouble believing that!"

Gabriela opened her mouth to question this somewhat disrespectful view of heavenly beings. Snarky, indeed! But she caught herself in time.

"What I meant was, do angels come down *today* to help us?" Olivia pushed the late bite of her muffin into her mouth, chewed, and swallowed. "Do you think one came to help Great-grandfather?"

"I honestly don't know," Janie confessed. "He'd been under tremendous pressure that day when he found out that Uncle Billy had lost all that money. And mother told me he'd been drinking that night at Martini's Place. Plus, he may have struck his head and passed out when he hit that tree with his car. He may have dreamed the whole thing. But Daddy believed to his dying day that his guardian angel came down to help him that night."

"Wouldn't it be cool if an angel appeared to one of us?" Olivia asked, her face lighting up at the thought.

Friday, December 21, 2007

Chapter 26

Amanda tossed a bright red sweater into her suitcase. She thought of her parents, who now lived in Italy. They would probably call her on Christmas Eve. They'd be surprised to hear that she and the children were spending the holidays in Bedford Falls. If George didn't show up, she would keep that to herself.

Amanda thought of gifts she would need to buy for the Bailey clan. As an only child whose parents traveled the world, she had fallen in love with Bedford Falls and George's big family. How many Bailey relatives and in-laws were there now, she wondered, counting up in her head. Just over sixty, including the West Coast Baileys and not counting the Hatches. At any rate, there would be plenty of other children for Peter and Marianne to play with.

Well, there was no time to buy presents for them. She'd have to give them gift cards. Kids usually liked those, anyway. Amanda had already wrapped gifts for her own children, and she now loaded them into a second suitcase.

Yesterday had been difficult. She and George had accompanied their son to court. The press had indeed gotten wind of the story, and filmed them entering the courthouse. Then they'd had to sit in the courtroom, which was filled with teenagers and adults who'd run afoul of the law. Some of them smelled. Others seemed to have a hard time staying awake. In the back were the reporters, eagerly awaiting the fate of George Bailey's son.

In the end – since George had refused to press charges against his son for breaking windows in his building – the judge had given him a lecture about his underage drinking and being out so late at night, and let him off. He would not even have to do community service, as this was his first offense. As they left the courtroom, Amanda wondered if the folks in Bedford Falls would hear of it.

"Are you two ready to go?" she called to Peter and Marianne.

"Yes, Mommy," Marianne replied, dragging her little pink suitcase on wheels into her mother's bedroom.

"Come here, sweetheart, and let me put your hair in a ponytail." Amanda brushed Marianne's silky blonde hair into place and slid an elastic band around it.

"There you go," she said. She suddenly realized that she had not seen Marianne smile in days.

"Is anything wrong, sweetheart?" she asked, pulling Marianne up onto her lap.

Marianne looked up at her.

"Daddy's not coming, is he?"

Amanda hesitated. She had no idea what George would do. She pressed her chin against Marianne's head, avoiding those questioning blue eyes. "He's going to try to come later, on Christmas Eve," she answered.

Chapter 27

Zuzu Bailey Brown pushed her shopping cart out of the grocery store and headed for her car, parked near the courthouse. Opening the back door, she unloaded bag after bag of food, most of it intended for the big Christmas Eve dinner when the family gathered at the Bailey house. She slammed the door shut and thought for a moment. It was only about 10 a.m. Did she have time for a little last-minute Christmas shopping before going home to read to Mary?

Yes, she decided. She'd stop at Gower Drugs, which carried toys and games this time of year, to look for something for Marianne and Peter. Zuzu hated the big, ugly toy store just outside of town, the one that had put the little Bedford Falls toy shop out of business. If she wanted toys for her grandchildren, Zuzu bought them online – something her granddaughter Ashley had taught her to do.

As she shut the door of her car, Zuzu suddenly remembered she also needed to pick up Mary's new meds. She began walking down the long, tree-lined boulevard that was Genesee Street, towards Gower Drugs.

Glancing over at the Mongoose bar, Zuzu sighed sadly, remembering how the town had looked when she was a little girl. She could remember when the space the bar now occupied had been the county gas company. The library was still there on the corner, thank goodness, next to the Tip Top Cafe. Her father had spent so much time there as a young man, reading about all the places he'd wanted to visit.

Zuzu passed the space that had been the little Dance Academy, on the corner of Genesee and Washington. It was long gone, replaced, most recently, by a pizzeria.

Across the street, on the same block, had been a bowling alley and pool hall, where Daddy had spent occasional Saturday afternoons shooting pool with his friends. The pool hall had been replaced by that despicable men's club. Martini's Place had moved from its original location a few streets over to the corner of Genesee and Washington.

The old garage was long gone; it was now an electronic game store, part of a national chain. The Liberty Bicycle Shop, where Zuzu's father had bought his children their first bicycles, was also gone, its space now occupied by a bookstore, also part of a big national chain.

The old Bedford Falls *Sentinel* was still there, sharing quarters now with a UPS store. The old meat market was now a frozen yogurt shop. And next to that was the dear old Bailey Brothers Building and Loan. It had originally occupied the building's second floor, above Anderson's clothing store, but when Anderson's went out of business, the Building and Loan had expanded to both floors.

The light turned green; Zuzu crossed Washington Avenue, still recalling the businesses of her childhood. The Bedford Falls Trust and Savings Bank was the first building on the next block. It had been there since the early part of the last century. Zuzu recalled the stories her father had told her about the battles between Old Man Potter and Zuzu's grandfather, and the even more intense battles between Potter and Daddy.

Zuzu smiled, remembering her darling father. She'd been his pet, the only child he'd given a nickname to. She remembered how she used to climb on his back, her arms tight around his neck, while he pretended he didn't know she was there, and went about his business, walking out to pick up the newspaper and sitting down to read it.

Zuzu pulled her coat zipper higher as a gust of wind swept down the street, blowing snowflakes into her face. The old Bedford Falls Emporium had been right there, Zuzu remembered, where a Dillard's department store now stood. The old Western Union building was now a dry cleaners, but the barbershop was still there. Next door, Violet Bick's beauty shop had shared space with a florist's shop. A styling salon stood there now, currently running a pre-Christmas sale on coloring, Zuzu noticed.

At the corner of Genesee and Jefferson, Zuzu waited for the light to turn, and then crossed Jefferson. Facing her was the old Bedford House hotel, although it, too, had undergone many changes in ownership and had been remodeled several times. Zuzu was glad it had managed to escape the fate of so many other Bedford Falls businesses – that of being converted into just another anonymous unit of a national or even international chain.

Next to the hotel, the family-owned bakery that had gone out of business a few years ago was still empty space. The wall between the old antique shop and Joe Hapner's luggage and sporting goods store had been knocked down to make way for the Kingfish Saloon. *Dear old Joe Hapner*, Zuzu thought fondly. Her father had finally used that suitcase – the one Mr. Gower had bought for him – on the trip he and Mother had taken to Europe eighteen years after Daddy had received it.

Gower Drugs was directly opposite Zuzu on the other side of Genesee. *Let's see*, she thought: *That cell phone store used to be a candy shop, and that home-decorating business was once the Jenkins Art Store. And what did that taekwondo gym used to be? Oh, yes, the McKenzie Music Store.* The McKenzies still lived in Bedford Falls, but Zuzu wasn't sure what line of business the younger generations were involved in.

The Bijou Theatre was still there. Both Janie and Zuzu made sure the town kept the agreement demanded by their father when he gave the theater to Bedford Falls, that only films suitable for families be shown there. Janie glanced up at the billboard and smiled. *Ratatouille*, about a rat who liked to cook, was now playing. She made a mental note to take Marianne to see it when she arrived. Peter probably considered himself too old to see a children's film, but she'd invite him, just the same.

Gower Drugs was next door to the theater, on the corner. Zuzu pushed open the door, taking pleasure in the warm air that swept over her.

"Hi, Travis!" she called to Travis Gower, the current owner of Gower Drugs. "Are my mother's meds ready?"

Old Emil Gower had died when Zuzu was entering her teens. He'd been a sweet old man who never failed to give her a free lollipop or Hershey bar when she came in. He didn't do this with her friends, and she had sometimes wondered why he seemed to be so fond of the Bailey family. Maybe Daddy had done something for him once, Zuzu thought. He'd done thoughtful things for so many people.

One of Mr. Gower's nephews had taken over the drug store in the 1950s and modernized it. But he, too, had passed on, and his son Travis – much younger than Zuzu, as everybody seemed to be these days – was now behind the counter.

Zuzu turned to the toy aisle. Within fifteen minutes, she had chosen board games for the kids – Galaxy Trucker for Peter, and Zooloretto for

Marianne – had them gift-wrapped, and picked up Mary's meds.

Zuzu pushed open the door, a great cold *whoosh* of cold air hitting her face.

Impulsively, she decided to visit the Building and Loan and see how things were going. It was just across the street, and she was still on the board of directors – the only Bailey to hold such a position. She knew the current manager, Jordan Lake, but she didn't know most of the new people very well, although she made a point of meeting each new employee.

Zuzu entered the bank's spacious lobby. Two people she didn't know were standing at the teller's window. She climbed the stairs to the second floor with an effort, her arthritic knees giving her trouble. The offices were up here. In the second floor lobby, Zuzu dropped down onto a sofa. Unzipping her coat, she glanced up at the paintings of her father and grandfather hanging on the wall facing her. Zuzu's late husband had painted them.

Zuzu wondered if Jordan Lake would have time to visit with her today. She heard the soft buzz of voices in Uncle Billy's old office – Carl Sanderson's office now. A young Latina woman was seated nearby, holding a baby while a toddler played at her feet.

A moment later, a young man left Carl Sanderson's office. He walked over to the young woman, who looked up at him eagerly. He shook his head.

The young woman burst into tears. "Hush," the young man whispered, putting his arm around her. "We knew it was a long shot. We'll try again next year."

The children, upset by their mother's sobs, began to cry, too. "Let's go," the man said, picking up the toddler.

"Wait a minute," Zuzu heard herself saying.

The couple looked at her in surprise. Zuzu, embarrassed, was not sure what to say.

"My name is Elizabeth Bailey Brown," she said finally. "My grandfather and his brother started this Building and Loan. I was just wondering...well, if there was something I could do for you."

The young man's smile held a touch of bitterness. "Not unless you can change Mr. Sanderson's mind. He just turned down my loan request. We were hoping to buy a house in Bailey Park. It's one of the smaller ones. The owners just moved out and put it up for sale."

"Did he say why he turned down the loan?" Zuzu asked.

"He said I was a bad risk. I do seasonal work, mostly – picking fruit and vegetables in the summer. I also work as a handyman. I do a lot of repairs for my neighbors. And I've been selling Christmas trees since just after Thanksgiving."

"Where do you live now, if I may ask?"

"With my folks," the young man replied. "But it's getting too crowded for us."

"I can imagine," Zuzu agreed, smiling down at the children. "By the way, what are your names?"

"I'm Joaquin Cruz, he replied. "And this is my wife, Anna, and our son, Jordi and our daughter" – pointing to the baby – "Emmanuela."

"Was she born at Christmas?" Zuzu asked, smiling. The baby appeared to be about a year old.

"Yes, on Christmas Day last year. Right after my wife had cooked mountains of food!"

Both Joaquin and Anna smiled a bit sadly. Suddenly, into Zuzu's mind, came the words her father had spoken to Old Man Potter on the day he'd intended to leave for college and the beginning of a life outside Bedford Falls. She had not witnessed this little drama, but Uncle Billy had told her the story over and over again, with great relish.

Old Man Potter had just criticized her father for authorizing a loan to Ernie Bishop, the town's taxi driver and George Bailey's close friend. Potter had sarcastically told the board, "You see, if you shoot pool with some employee here, you can come and borrow money. What does that get us? A discontented, lazy rabble instead of a thrifty working class. And all because a few starry-eyed dreamers like Peter Bailey stir them up and fill their heads with a lot of impossible ideas..."

According to Uncle Billy, her outraged father had interrupted Potter and put him in his place. The words were engraved in Zuzu's memory:

"Do you know how long it takes a working man to save five thousand dollars? Just remember this, Mr. Potter, that this rabble you're talking about, they do most of the working and paying and living and dying in this community. Well, is it too much to have them work and pay and live and die in a couple of decent rooms and a bath? Anyway, my father didn't think so. People were human beings to him, but to you, a warped, frustrated old man, they're cattle..."

Zuzu made up her mind.

"You stay right here," she ordered. "Sit down. I'm going to have a word with Mr. Sanderson."

The Cruzes obediently sat down as Zuzu walked to the door of Uncle Billy's old office and knocked.

"Why, Mrs. Brown!" Mr. Sanderson said. He rose politely, came round his big desk, and took Zuzu's hand. "How very nice to see you. Can I be of service to you?"

"Yes," Zuzu said bluntly. "I want you to approve a loan for that nice young couple, the Cruzes. They're still here."

The smile stayed on Mr. Sanderson's face, but no longer quite reached his eyes. "Mrs. Brown, as much as I'd like to do that, the risk to the Building and Loan is just too great. Why – "

"I know all about the Cruzes," Zuzu interrupted. "I know he doesn't have a permanent, full-time job. Given the economy, I'm not surprised. But he clearly works hard. All you have to do is look at him to see what a decent, trustworthy, hard-working man he is – "

"But Mrs. Brown – "

"He has a wife and two small children. They're crowded into a little house with relatives – "

"But Mrs. Brown – "

Zuzu smiled to take the sting out of her next words. "Mr. Sanderson, I'm not leaving this building until that couple has their loan. If you won't approve it, I'll have to take it up with Mr. Lake. I'm still on the board of directors, you know."

Mr. Sanderson sighed and looked into Zuzu's determined face. "I'm afraid that's what you're going to have to do, Mrs. Brown. I just follow the rules. I don't make them."

An hour later, Zuzu, accompanied by a very happy Cruz family, left the Building and Loan. Zuzu couldn't help the grin spreading across her own face. Jordan Lake had put up a fight. Oh, yes, he had. But when Zuzu threatened to bring the entire Bailey clan downtown to pay him a visit (after stopping at the Bedford Falls *Sentinel* to invite a reporter to come with them), he'd finally backed down.

Zuzu's grin faded as she waved goodbye to the Cruzes. What had happened to the Building and Loan? Her father would have given the Cruzes a loan in a heartbeat. But then, her father, like his father before him, had always based his decisions more on a customer's character than the amount of money in his bank account. Clearly, this was no longer being done.

Zuzu decided to visit the Building and Loan a little more often. And perhaps, she mused, it was time for a Bailey or two to work there again.

She gave a final wave to the Cruz family and, turning right, headed back up Genesee to the Courthouse parking lot. Three minutes later, as she was opening her car door, she felt her purse being yanked off her arm. Frightened, Zuzu turned around in time to see a young man running away with it.

Chapter 28

At the police station, Zuzu told an officer what had happened, giving the best description she could of the purse snatcher: a slender young man wearing a black coat and a black-and-red ski cap.

Zuzu was still trembling from the shock. She was not as upset about losing her cash as she was that such a thing had happened in Bedford Falls. She had never been victimized by crime before, but in the space of a few days, she and Janie had both experienced unpleasant attacks.

A few hours later, Officer Kennedy called Zuzu to let her know they'd found her purse lying in some bushes. Her money and credit cards were gone. Zuzu had, of course, canceled her credit cards the minute she got home, but the young thief had already used one at the big grocery store just outside of town. Security cameras confirmed the identity of the person who'd used it: Jeremy Blake, a seventeen-year-old student at Bedford Falls High School. ' "We have him here at the station," Officer Kennedy told Zuzu.

"Did he say why he did it?"

"Yeah. He says his dad spent all of his money on one of those grocery store lottery machines and then took off. The kid said he needed money to buy food for his younger brothers and sister."

Zuzu, staring out the living room window as the snow fell, sighed as she thought again about how much Bedford Falls had changed. Irrelevantly, she remembered that Officer Kennedy's grandparents had taken out a loan for their house in Bailey Park during the 1930s. She wondered who lived there now.

Officer Kennedy waited for Zuzu to respond. Finally, he said, "Do you want to press charges?"

Zuzu hesitated, thinking of her father.

"Is this his first offense?"

"Yeah."

"I don't think I want to press charges. He didn't hurt me. But I would like to talk to him."

Chapter 29

It took Amanda five hours to drive from Manhattan to Bedford Falls, the children playing with their Gameboys in the backseat of her black BMW. She had waited for morning rush hour traffic to subside before starting out. The weather forecast had been for mixed rain and snow, but as she approached Bedford Falls, it began to snow in earnest. Clearly, it had been snowing for days; the roads had been cleared over and over again, and the piles of dirty snow lining the sides of the highway were at least six feet high.

"Hey, look at all this snow!" Amanda said to her children.

"Yeah," Peter responded, not looking up from his Gameboy.

Amanda knew both the children were nervous over the tension between their parents this week; they sensed that something was badly wrong. Although Amanda had told Peter and Marianne that their father would follow them to Bedford Falls if he could, she knew they were not fooled. Dad was almost certainly not coming for Christmas.

Amanda hoped they had not caught television reports regarding the worst of what was going on with Bailey Investments. Shame, combined with the anger they already felt towards him, would permanently warp their relationship with him. Both of them had already been teased at school about their father, "Scrooge Bailey."

Through the slapping wipers, Amanda spotted the slightly dilapidated sign signaling the end of their journey: "You are now in Bedford Falls." But the stab of joy she always felt when returning to her adopted hometown was missing this time. Amanda was simply relieved that the long trip was over.

She turned the car onto Washington Street. Glancing around as she drove, Amanda found even more changes than she'd seen during her last visit six months previously. Somebody had opened up a new Indian curry takeout shop. As she reached the intersection of Washington and Genesee, she spotted a blinking Schlitz sign. Had that bar been there before? she wondered. How many taverns did one small town need?

Amanda drove several more blocks into the residential section of town and turned onto Sycamore Street. Her spirits lifted slightly as she saw the old Bailey house. Pulling into the driveway, she parked behind Zuzu's old mini-van – the one with "Zuzu's Petals" and an image of a single red rose painted on the side.

The children, excited now they were here, climbed out the car and ran up the walk to the front door. Marianne raised her hand to push the doorbell, but Aunt Zuzu had heard their car pull up. She opened the door with a delighted smile.

"Hello, you two!" she greeted them. "Come in and have some cookies and hot chocolate. Hi, Amanda," she added, as their mother came up behind the children. Zuzu stood on tiptoe to kiss Amanda's cheek as Peter and Marianne raced into the kitchen.

"Where's George?"

Chapter 30

Janie Bailey Martini sat before her grand piano, playing "I Heard the Bells on Christmas Day." As usual, she'd been asked to perform special music at the Christmas Eve service at the Presbyterian church.

Janie thought back on the great performance halls in which she'd performed in New York, Rome, London, and Sydney. She smiled a little, remembering those days. These days, she was content to play for the citizens of Bedford Falls, people she had known and loved since childhood, and their children and grandchildren.

She glanced up at the portrait of her father, which hung over the fireplace. *Eighteen years*, she thought. *You've been gone almost two decades.*

Her mother had taught Janie to love God, but it was her father who had taught her to love her neighbors. And to Janie, everyone she encountered was a neighbor. Her father's example was the reason she'd been willing to play so many benefit concerts over the years, and why she'd returned to Bedford Falls when she retired. Family, friends, and community were everything, her father had told her; never underestimate your need for them, or theirs for you.

Janie switched to another carol and began singing softly, "Hark the herald angels sing..."

It was the first Christmas carol she'd ever learned.

She heard Roberto banging the snow off his boots outside. He opened the kitchen door and came in. Janie stood up to greet him – still the handsomest man she knew – and he swung her into a hug.

"They're here," he told her. "I just saw Amanda's car pull into your mother's driveway."

Chapter 31

Zuzu handed Amanda a tissue and looked sympathetically at her niece by marriage.

"And so you finally had enough," she said.

"Yes. I couldn't bear it any longer." Amanda wiped her eyes. "He said he'd try to make it for Christmas, but I think he was just trying to get me to leave him alone about it. I don't think he's going to be here."

"Let me make you a cup of tea," Zuzu said. "Why don't you come into the kitchen with me? It's warmer there. I've been baking cookies all afternoon."

"George has always been too fond of making money, but in the last year or so, he's become so obsessed with it that he no longer has time for the children. Or for me," Amanda said as she followed Zuzu to the kitchen. "And the decisions he's been making lately have hurt a lot of people."

"Yes," Zuzu murmured. "I've been watching it on television."

Amanda's head snapped up. "Does Mary know about that poor woman who killed herself?"

"Yes," Zuzu responded. "She knows."

Chapter 32

*M*ary opened her eyes. The door to her bedroom was being quietly opened. A moment later, Amanda's sleek blonde head appeared.

Mary smiled. "Amanda!"

Amanda bent to kiss Mary's cheek and sat down next to the bed. She took Mary's hand.

"I hear you haven't been feeling too well," Amanda said.

"I'm much better now," Mary lied. Then, eagerly, she asked, "Did George come with you?"

Amanda's smile faded. "No, the children and I arrived early. He's hoping – planning – to come on Christmas Eve."

Mary searched Amanda's face, but did not comment on this. She knew as well as Amanda that George could not be relied upon to put family ahead of business. Her thoughts wandered into the past, thinking of how George came to them as a shattered fourteen-year-old, and how hard his grandfather had tried to get him to care about others. Now, she wondered how George had managed to marry someone as caring as Amanda.

"He was always a little on the selfish side," Mary murmured.

"What was that?" Amanda asked.

"Nothing. Tell me how the children are."

"Peter loves football. His team made it to the championship game this year." Amanda omitted to add that Peter, angry at his father's absence, had likely caused his team to lose.

"And Marianne loves her teacher this year. She had a big part in the school play. I sent you pictures, didn't I?"

"Yes. She was adorable. She reminds me of when Zuzu was a little girl, so enthusiastic about life."

Amanda thought of how down Marianne had been during the last few weeks, and the cause of it. Mary looked at her speculatively.

"Things aren't going well at home, are they?" she asked.

Amanda gave her a level look. "No, Mary, they're not. George doesn't spend any time with the children anymore. All he seems to care about is piling up more and more money. I'm afraid – "

"What are you afraid of, Amanda?"

"I'm afraid he's going to have to pay a terrible price someday for the way he's living his life."

Chapter 33

Zuzu opened the door to a thin young man, looking down at his shoes.

Jeremy Blake?" she asked.

"Yeah," he muttered.

"Come in."

The young man entered the house, and Zuzu invited him to sit on the sofa. She sat down herself and crossed her legs.

"Suppose you tell me why you stole my purse," Zuzu said. She spoke in a friendly way, but the boy didn't look up.

"My dad gambled away his paycheck and took off," Jeremy said, still looking down at his shoes. "We ran out of food at home. I needed money to buy more."

"You have three younger siblings, I believe?"

"Yeah."

"Have you thought about getting an after-school job?"

"Yeah, well, I tried, but we ran out of food before I could find one."

"What about your mother? Is it possible for her to go to work?"

"No. She's sick."

"What about relatives? Can they help you?"

"We don't have any relatives in Bedford Falls."

"What about going to a church and asking for help?"

"We don't go to church."

Zuzu sighed. "You don't have to belong to a church to go to one and tell them your family is in trouble. That's partly what churches are for: to help people who need it."

"I didn't know that."

"I didn't press charges against you because Officer Kennedy told me about you and your family situation," Zuzu said. "But there's still the matter of the $147 you put on my credit card."

"Yeah, I know."

"Jeremy."

The boy finally looked up at her.

"What do you say about working it off? You could shovel my front walkway, for instance. My brother Tommy is getting beyond jobs like that. And you could find ways to help the sexton at my church – or another church, if you prefer. Shoveling is hard work, so I'll deduct what you owe me at the rate of $10 per hour. How does that sound?"

"Sounds okay."

Zuzu was reluctant to ask Jeremy if he thought his father would return. If he did not, the problem of how to pay the bills at the Blake house would be a long-term one. She would put the family in touch with one of the service teams at church. Meanwhile – she thought again of her father, and of what he might do in this situation.

Zuzu got up, went to her father's old desk, and pulled out her checkbook. She filled out a check, tore it out, and handed it to Jeremy.

"This is for Christmas presents for your younger sister and brothers," she said.

Chapter 34

"Can we go to that Indian takeout place for dinner?" Peter looked at Amanda hopefully.

"They'll deliver," Zuzu told Amanda.

Amanda considered. She needed to get out of the house, and so did the kids. "I think I'd rather go there," she said. "What do you want me to bring you?"

"Mr. Chaudhury's Prawn Fry." Zuzu grinned.

Twenty minutes later, Amanda and her children were sitting at a tiny table at the Bombay Curry Cottage, waiting for their orders. Amanda glanced around at the framed posters of India. She could smell spicy food and hear Indian music filling the room.

"Look!" Marianne said excitedly, pointing to the wall behind Amanda's chair. Amanda twisted around and looked. She was startled to see a framed, black-and-white photograph of her husband's grandfather.

"It's Great-grandpa!" Marianna said excitedly.

"Now, I wonder why a takeout restaurant has a picture of him on the wall," Amanda said, almost to herself.

"I can tell you that," said a young man carrying steaming plates of chicken curry, rice, pita bread, and Cokes. He set them down on their table.

"My father and mother opened a restaurant twenty-five years ago, in 1982. But they had to close down after just a few months when my father was diagnosed with multiple sclerosis. We kids weren't old enough to help my mom keep the restaurant open, so it had to close."

The young man reached into his apron pocket, brought out straws, and handed one to each of them.

"We'd taken out a big loan from the Building and Loan, but there was no way we were going to pay it back with Pop getting sicker every day. Mom started cleaning houses just to pay for groceries. One of the houses she cleaned for years during the eighties was George and Mary Bailey's house. Mr. Bailey always wanted to know all about people, and when he found out about my dad, and the restaurant, and the loan, do you know what he did?"

Amanda was pretty sure she did.

"He paid off the loan himself," the young man said. "When my brothers and I got a little older, we all got after-school jobs to help Mom make ends meet every month.

"Mr. Bailey kept in touch with us over the years, and he fixed it so my three brothers and I were able to go to college with scholarships from the Bailey Family Trust. I went to the Culinary Institute of America. And then I came back here and bought this place. I'll be back in a second."

The young man left the table and brought orders to two other customers, then returned to Amanda.

"This little restaurant may not look like much now, but my wife and I plan to expand it in a few years. I've never forgotten George Bailey's generosity. I wish he'd lived to see this place. I'd have given him a free meal every single day."

He glanced up at the framed picture of George Bailey, taken when he was around seventy.

"And as long as I live, I'm going to make sure other people don't forget George Bailey's generosity, either."

"What's your name?" Amanda asked.

"Jagan Chaudhury."

Chapter 35

"*Dear Aunt Zuzu,* George wrote. *Thanks for your note and the update on Grandmother.*

About the hospital – Amanda and I just gave ten million dollars to the Castlebury Museum. We can't possibly make any additional donations at present. I know you will understand.

Say hello to Grandmother for me.

– George

Saturday, December 22, 2007

Chapter 36

Amanda, Peter, Marianne stood on the sidewalk watching the annual Christmas parade straggle down Genesee. Beside them were Janie, her son Ed and daughter-in-law Sophia, and their four youngsters, ranging from ten-year-old Tyler to two-year-old Caitlin. Ed held his youngest up high so she could see over the people in front of them, and put his arm around the shivering Sophia, who was six months pregnant with their fifth child.

Everything Amanda loved about small-town parades was present today. The floats were unsophisticated, the costumes homemade, and roughly half of the children of Bedford Falls were taking part.

Sara Martini, the eight-year-old daughter of Nicky and Julia Martini, was dressed up as a snowflake. Martin Hatch, Jr., Mary Bailey's seventy-four-year-old nephew, was dressed as Santa Claus. He threw candy canes from a cart drawn by a tired-looking white pony with a wreath around its neck.

The Bedford High School Band was blasting out "Jingle Bells" and "Here Comes Santa Claus" as its members marched down the street. Two children began squabbling over a candy cane. A dog cocked his leg and relieved itself in the already dirty snow at the foot of a telephone pole. A small boy dressed as one of Santa's elves suddenly tripped and fell against another elf, knocking both of them to the street, where they began punching each other. Their mothers ran out to separate them.

New York City had nothing on this, Amanda thought in amusement.

Amanda knew Peter didn't want to watch the parade – he was sulking, and refusing to talk to anyone. But Marianne was loving it. Her great-uncle Tommy had decided to accompany them to the parade. Now, he hoisted Marianne on his shoulders so she could see better. Amanda took their picture. Uncle Tommy might not be the most successful member of the family, Amanda thought, but he had a kind heart. She thought of George, and tears stung her eyes. She needed to be around someone with a kind heart just now. So did the children.

The parade scraggled to a finish. The crowd cheered and clapped. Janie turned to Amanda and Sophia. "Shall we go to the restaurant and get warmed up?"

"Yey!" the children whooped. The restaurant meant fun with their uncles and Grandfather Roberto, sweet rolls and hot chocolate, and maybe pizza for an early lunch.

"Let's go!" shouted four-year-old Isabella.

Sunday, December 23, 2007

Chapter 37

It was the fourth Sunday of Advent. At the Bedford Falls Presbyterian Church, Amanda Bailey sat in the third pew from the front, Marianne on one side, Zuzu on the other. Peter had flatly refused to attend, and Amanda had finally given up and left him with Mary, Makina, and Uncle Tommy.

Janie's children and grandchildren lined the pew in front of Amanda, the younger ones squirming and giggling so loudly that Janie, softly playing the prelude on the organ, could hear them. Gabriela was seated next to her husband, James Townsend. Their own three daughters sat next to them, wearing dresses under protest. Various other relatives filled out the pew.

After the minister welcomed the congregation, Janie began "O Come, All Ye Faithful," and the congregation rose to sing. sf Amanda loved the ancient Advent hymns, but she could not enjoy them today. *Oh, George*, she thought sadly. Amanda wondered if the two of them would still be together in the coming year. George, the tall, handsome man who had swept her off her feet fourteen years ago.

What had made him change so drastically? And how could she bring back the man he'd once been, the man who, despite everything, she still deeply loved?

Chapter 38

Zuzu was in the kitchen, helping Makina wash up a few dishes. Tommy was at the kitchen table, reading the newspaper. They all started as several sets of knuckles began pounding on the front door of Mary Bailey's house. Someone was repeatedly ringing the doorbell.

Zuzu smiled as she went to answer the door. It could only be –

"Merry Christmas!" shouted around two dozen West Coast Baileys.

"Merry Christmas, darlings!" Zuzu cried, as her cousins swarmed in to hug and kiss her. "About time you got here!"

"Our flight was delayed in Chicago," Walter Bailey explained. "Otherwise, we would have been here hours ago."

The families always made a point of joining up in Chicago so they could fly the rest of the way – to New York, then Rochester, and then Bedford Falls – together.

Walter dumped a sack of gaily wrapped presents under the Christmas tree. "We almost left these at the airport."

"Well, your rooms are ready. Do you want something to eat?"

Zuzu gazed fondly at Uncle Harry's descendants. Harry Bailey, her father's much-loved brother, had died in 1997, aged 87 years. He had never returned to Bedford Falls to live, but after serving in the war, Harry had returned to work in research and development at his father-in-law's glass company in Buffalo, some one hundred and fifteen miles west of Bedford Falls. It was close enough so that Harry and George and their families could frequently visit each other.

Harry and his wife, Ruth, had had three children. They had all married and had children of their own, and some of those children were now parents themselves.

Amanda emerged from the kitchen with a tray of tall glasses.

"Merry Christmas! Have some eggnog."

Zuzu eyed her. Clearly, Amanda was determined to put on a happy face. Good for her.

"Amanda! Good to see you," said Walter, bending to kiss her. "Where's George?"

Chapter 39

*I*n his New York penthouse, George felt a sense of uneasiness. It was so quiet with Amanda and the children gone – not a good quiet, but a slightly ominous one.

He poured himself his usual evening drink, and wandered about the living room. He walked over to his wall safe, opened it, and pulled out the black velvet box. It contained his Christmas gift to Amanda: A necklace that matched the sapphire and diamond earrings and bracelet he'd already given her. He suddenly wondered why he had bought it. She never asked for jewelry, and didn't seem to value it the way he did.

But if he didn't give her jewelry, what *could* he give her? His mind explored this idea as he wandered around the apartment. Perhaps they could go on a trip together when things let up at the office. Perhaps a tour through Asia.

As he finished his drink, George wondered what Amanda was doing right now. And – as had happened several times in the last few days – he felt a sense of dread shoot through him.

Chapter 40

The Baileys, Hatches, Martinis, Browns, their children, grandchildren, and various in-laws, were lined up in the first three rows of chairs in the basement of the Presbyterian Church, amused smiles on their faces. On stage before them, the children of the church, including a number of Bailey kids, were performing the Christmas story.

Janie had come early with her brood to secure good seats. Now, she watched tensely as her four-year-old granddaughter, Charlotte, playing an angel, swung into view above a neon-green field, where three shepherd boys were watching their flocks by night. Janie hoped her skinny granddaughter would not slip out of the rope, or forget her lines. Which were coming up right now.

"Do not be afraid, 'cuz I'm bringing you good news!" Charlotte hollered down to the shepherds.

Little Isabella, seated in the front row, burst into giggles.

"Hush!" Sophia whispered to her.

"Today, in the town of David, a Savior has been born. He is the Messiah, the Lord."

Well, she got that part right, anyway, thought Janie, smiling.

Charlotte began to swing a bit as she tried to remember her last line.

"Here's how you find him: Go to the manger and he's lying there in some straw."

Several adults in the audience smothered chuckles. The curtains abruptly closed, then opened again on the manger scene. The angel had disappeared, replaced by a large foil star that had been hoisted above the manger.

The shepherds entered from the left, got down on their knees, and admired the baby who was indeed lying in the straw, kicking his fat legs. As the straw began working its way under his clothing, he began to wail. The actors said their last lines and then invited the audience to sing "Away in a Manger" with them.

And then the curtain closed on the children's Christmas program of 2007.

Monday, December 24, 2007

Chapter 41
7 a.m.

The morning of Christmas Eve dawned. Dark clouds filled with snow banked over Bedford Falls. Residents looked up at the sky and shook their heads. When, they wondered, would it stop snowing? Living in upstate New York, they knew it was unreasonable to expect tropical weather in December. But this was too much. There hadn't been this much snow since the winter of 1912, according to the almanac. Weather forecasters were predicting a blizzard late today, with up to two feet of snow.

As Bedford Fallsians bundled up once more and made their way to work, a sudden wind whipped up, and then, strangely, it stopped. Walking to his part-time job selling Christmas trees, Joaquin Cruz looked around uneasily. The town and the mountains surrounding it seemed to have a queer air of suspense.

And not a nice, Christmassy sense of suspense, Zuzu thought, flicking the curtains closed again. The town seemed to be waiting for something to happen. Something menacing.

Chapter 42
7:30 a.m.

George Bailey remembered the moment he awoke that he had an important decision to make. Should he call the Kaufmans and the De Lucas and tell them he'd join them on December 26 instead of this evening?

It was going to look bad enough that Amanda wasn't coming. Perhaps he could fly the company jet to Bedford Falls this afternoon, spend the evening and Christmas morning with the family, and then fly out at noon for Vermont. As he rose and prepared coffee, George wondered if that would be enough for Amanda.

At 8 a.m., his cell phone rang. It was Aaron Kaufman.

"George!"

Kaufman, a member of the New York City Department of Planning, greeted him heartily. "I'm calling from Sugarbush. The kids were after us to leave early, so Roz and I decided to fly the family up here yesterday. We can't wait for you and Amanda to get here."

George said nothing. *What was he going to do?*

"You're still coming tonight, aren't you?" asked the man who had the power to either approve or shut down the future plans of Bailey Investments.

George suddenly made up his mind. "Yes, I'll be there tonight," he said.

Chapter 43
11:59 a.m.

In her new apartment on the sixth floor of the McClure building, Tamera Bradshaw was preparing lunch for her children. Gracie was playing with blocks nearby, and Conner was playing electronic games on the TV.

Tamera heated homemade tomato soup, spread peanut butter on whole wheat bread, and sliced an apple. After lunch, Tamera planned to take the children to explore a nearby park.

They had been in the new apartment for three days and everything had finally been unpacked, unrolled, put away, or hung up. As she worked, Tamera took quick, happy glances at the black granite counter tops, the blue Thai silk window treatments, and the new Oriental rug in the living room. It was the home she and Spencer had been dreaming of since Conner had been born. She smiled a smile of pure happiness.

Conner, tiring of his game, came into the kitchen.

"Let's find something to do," he said to Gracie.

His little sister put down her blocks agreeably and went with her brother into the living room.

As Tamera began putting the lunch dishes on the dining room table, she felt the apartment shake slightly. One of the children's favorite games was jumping from sofa to chair to chair to sofa, in a circle, as fast as they could.

"Stop jumping on the furniture, kids!" she warned.

"We're not!" they yelled back.

Chapter 44
12:00 p.m.

The apartment continued to shake. Tamera looked up at the ceiling in alarm. What was going on? Nervous, she went into the living room to check on Gracie and Conner.

Suddenly a huge crack split the newly painted ceiling. Gracie screamed. And then with a roar, the ceiling, and the contents of the apartment above, collapsed on them.

Chapter 45
12:25 p.m.

George sipped his drink as he made a rough estimate of how many of his senior-level employees and their spouses had come to Bailey Investments' annual Christmas buffet lunch at the Plaza Hotel.

The Plaza was beautifully decorated for Christmas, and Bailey Investments had reserved a large room for their annual event. Two or three employees were drinking a little too much, George noticed, and many of the others lacked the enthusiasm he would have expected for an event with free booze and pricey little sandwiches and desserts. It did not occur to him that many of them might prefer to be home with their families, finishing up last-minute Christmas shopping, or getting an early start on a drive to the out-of-town home of relatives.

It did not occur to George that they might be afraid *not* to come.

George wondered where Ron Ayers was. He'd said he had several things to finish up in the office before taking a full week off for the holidays. George had let him know how inconvenient this was, but Ayers, surprisingly, had stood firm. He and his family were going to his sister's house in Connecticut for a week, and that was that. Maybe, George considered, it was time to look for a replacement for his assistant.

George felt a slight draft as someone opened the door to the room, and turned to see Ron stride in. George could see, even from a distance, that he was perspiring heavily and looking around urgently. George finished his drink, put down the glass, and strolled over to him.

"What's up?" he asked.

Ron swallowed. "I just got a call from the police. A chunk of the seventh floor of the McClure building just collapsed. We have two families living just below the collapsed part. One of them wasn't home, but the other family was hurt pretty bad. They're in the hospital."

George felt his stomach knot up.

"How many of them?"

"A mother and two little kids. I called someone I know at the hospital. She told me the mother has a lot of broken bones and a crushed pelvis. The little boy will probably be okay after some surgery. But the little girl – "

Ron did not want to continue. Fear rose up in George's chest.

"What about the little girl?"

"She may not live," Ron answered, looking at the floor. "Her skull was fractured."

Chapter 46
12:27 p.m.

Journalists lost no time hunting down the head of Bailey Investments. They knew his annual employee Christmas lunch took place at the Plaza. Moments after Ron had given George the bad news, a journalist managed to burst through the door of their private room, waving his cell phone camera in George's direction. Plaza security promptly grabbed him and began escorting him out, but not before he fired off a question for George.

"Mr. Bailey, do you have any comment to make about the collapse of the McClure building and the injuries suffered by the family living on the floor below?" he shouted.

The roomful of guests gasped. One of them dropped a china plate, which smashed noisily onto the floor. Everyone stared at George, who remained calm.

"Ron," he said, turning to his assistant. "Get a press release out expressing our dismay over what happened today, and announcing that Bailey Investments will launch a full investigation into why that building collapsed. Say we'll pay the hospital bills for everyone who was injured. And send flowers to all the family members, immediately."

Ron looked at him in disgust.

"Do it yourself."

George, who'd already begun to walk away, halted and turned to look coldly into Ron's face.

"What did you say?"

"I said, do it yourself. It's Christmas Eve. I have a family to go home to. And I'm resigning from Bailey Investments as of this minute. Clean up your own mess."

George's face reddened in fury. He opened his mouth to tell Ron what he thought of him, but too many employees were watching, some in shock, others with a certain look of satisfaction on their faces.

Ron turned and walked out of the room. George raised his voice to address his guests.

"Folks, I'm afraid I'm going to have to leave a bit early. I hope you'll all stay and enjoy your meal. Enjoy yourselves, everyone."

In a lower voice, he asked a waiter, "Where's the back door?"

"This way," he answered, jerking his head to the right. "I'll go with you, Mr. Bailey."

Chapter 47
12:27 p.m.

New York City reporters could hardly believe their luck. A big story like this on Christmas Eve! This beat silly stories about Santa sightings. A collapsed building, a kid in the hospital, maybe dying, and George Bailey, the real estate tycoon everybody loved to hate.

The reporters were not stupid. When George exited from a back door of the Plaza, a dozen of them were waiting for him, their cameras already running. A print photographer snapped a picture of George just as he looked up, startled.

"What construction company worked on the McClure Building?" a reporter shouted.

George inwardly cursed. He should have remembered to call Adrian and have him meet him at the back of the building. He couldn't go back inside; the door locked automatically. He pulled out his cell phone.

"Wasn't it Saunders Construction?" another journalist shouted as he jogged backwards to stay ahead of George.

More cameras clicked and flashed in the alley. George raised his arm before his eyes and walked faster. He punched his driver's speed dial number.

"Didn't Saunders build that hotel where a floor collapsed a couple of years ago?" another reporter yelled.

"Adrian, pick me up in front of the Plaza immediately," George instructed his driver. His long legs carried him rapidly around the corner to the front of the hotel. The pack of jackals followed.

"Mr. Bailey, what's the latest on those kids that were crushed? Are they gonna be okay?"

Some of the reporters had not yet heard about the Bradshaw family, and now they, too, began barking questions about the injured and their chances of survival. They knew George would not have this information, but it made for good television to ask him.

George spotted Adrian as he skillfully brought the limo to the curb despite the heavy late-afternoon traffic. George yanked open the door, got in, and slammed it shut.

"Take me home, Adrian," he ordered.

Chapter 48
1 p.m.

Zuzu could hear the faint sounds of the one o'clock news on her mother's television; the nurse had evidently turned it on before she left. Zuzu picked up the vase of flowers she'd been arranging and carried it to her mother's bedroom.

"Hi, Mom," she said, placing the vase on the bedside table. Impulsively, she bent to kiss her mother. "Would you like some cream of asparagus soup for dinner?"

But Mary Bailey was not listening. She was watching the television screen, which showed her grandson George as he walked rapidly down a New York City street, holding his arm up against the press of television cameras and shouting reporters. And then, images of the McClure building, with police cars, ambulances, and fire trucks out front. She watched as three paramedics carefully carried a stretcher out of the building and placed it in one of the ambulances. The small figure on the stretcher, viewers were told, was that of a four-year-old girl.

Oh, no, Zuzu thought. *George, what have you done?*

Chapter 49
1:17 p.m.

A mob of reporters was waiting on the sidewalk in front of the building where George lived. They immediately spotted George's car and began filming.

"Go around to the back," George ordered Adrian.

His driver obeyed. From inside the car, George watched as reporters began to run down the street. Adrian turned the corner, drove down the street, and turned again, dropping George off at a door in back. George managed to get inside just as the pack raced around the side of the building. But he was hardly free of them. His cell phone began ringing. Not recognizing the caller, George immediately cut off the call. Moments later, his phone rang again. It continued to ring as George rode up the elevator, unlocked the door of the duplex, and entered his glass-walled sanctuary. Shutting the door behind him, George turned off the phone.

Chapter 50
1:22 p.m.

"Why is Uncle George so mean?"

Harry Bailey's fourteen-year-old great-granddaughter, Kayla, was helping her great-aunt Zuzu peel potatoes and finish the pies for the Christmas Eve dinner before the entire Bailey clan headed for church.

Zuzu privately agreed that George was, indeed, rather mean, but she didn't want to say so to Kayla.

"What makes you say he's mean?" she said, beginning to roll out pastry.

"I saw on television that he kicked people out of one of those buildings he owns," Kayla replied, finishing one potato and picking up another. "And one of them killed herself."

Zuzu had no response to this observation. Like her mother, she had been dismayed when she'd heard the news – dismayed, but not surprised.

"I mean, doesn't he have enough money already?"

"Yes, he has a lot of money," Zuzu replied, dumping apple slices and cranberries into the pie shell. "More than any of us ever dreamed of having. More than my father ever had, and he had a lot," she added.

"Then why does Uncle George act like he doesn't have enough? Why can't he just stop making money and... you know, be nice to people? He could fix up that apartment building the way he wants and just let those old people live there until they die. And then – "

Kayla frowned, putting a crease above her pretty green eyes and freckled nose as she thought this through.

"And then he could let other people move in and charge THEM more, if he wanted to."

Kayla glanced up at her aunt, waiting for confirmation that she was on the right track – or not. Zuzu smiled down at her.

"You are one smart cookie, Kayla," she said. "And you have a good heart."

Unlike George, she thought sorrowfully.

Chapter 51
1:27 p.m.

George turned on his phone again, wanting to call Amanda and see how she and the kids were doing. It rang immediately. George recognized a Bailey Investments number and answered.

"Mr. Bailey?"

"Yes."

"It's Derek Adams. I work in public relations at Bailey Investments. Do you want me to put out a press release?"

He didn't have to explain why.

"Yes," George responded. "Just say we intend to get to the bottom of this, and that our prayers are with – "

"The Bradshaw family," Derek supplied.

"With the Bradshaw family. And that we'll pay the family's medical bills, and find them a place to live while the building is being repaired."

"I'm on it, sir. Anything else, sir?"

George suddenly remembered Ron's refusal to work that afternoon, and his stormy departure.

"Thanks for working so late on Christmas Eve," he said finally.

"No problem, sir. I'm Jewish."

Chapter 52
2 p.m.

Mary Bailey kept the television on, searching for any updates on what had happened to George's building. At two o'clock, the story led the news. Mary watched with growing fear as the anchor gave more details about the collapse of the top floor of the McClure building.

Mary could scarcely believe her eyes. George was responsible for this? For the terrible injuries, for that little girl struggling for her life in the hospital? How could her grandson, George Bailey's grandson, have come to build such shoddy apartments? Did money mean so much to him that he was willing to put lives at risk?

Mary suddenly remembered the story she'd seen on CNN a few days before, describing how an elderly woman had committed suicide when Bailey Investments had forced her out of her apartment of some sixty years. Bad as that was, today's catastrophe was far worse.

Oh, George, Mary thought despairingly, *You've turned into Henry Potter.*

She clicked off the television. Her heart pounding in her chest, Mary bowed her head and began to pray for the grandson who had inexplicably lost his way.

Chapter 53
2:30 p.m.

Makina washed her hands at the kitchen sink, untied her apron, and hung it up in the kitchen pantry. Zuzu was at the kitchen table, mashing together yams, eggs, brown sugar, and butter for a casserole.

"It's time for me to go pick up James from the babysitter. She didn't want to look after him too long today because she'd got her family coming for Christmas," Makina told Zuzu.

"Okay," Zuzu responded distractedly.

Makina put on her wool coat, covering the brightly patterned Nigerian dress she was wearing.

"I just checked on Mrs. Bailey. She seems kind of upset. She's been watching the TV all afternoon."

Zuzu met her eyes.

"She's upset about some news she heard today about her grandson," she said.

"Yes," I heard it on the radio," Makina said sympathetically. "Her grandson, he's in a lot of trouble, isn't he?"

Chapter 54
2:55 p.m.

"Amanda, I'd like to talk with you for a minute," Zuzu said.

Amanda was boiling cranberries, sugar, and orange peel for the cranberry sauce. She looked up questioningly. Zuzu could no longer put off telling Amanda about the building collapse; she or someone else in the house might turn on the three o'clock news.

"Come and sit down," she invited. "What's wrong?" Amanda asked, dropping down on a kitchen chair.

Zuzu told her.

Amanda stared at her, struggling to absorb what Zuzu was saying.

"Oh, dear Lord," she whispered.

She stood up, walked into the living room, and stood before the Christmas tree in the big front bay window. Its lights were still dark. Outside, the snow continued to fall. Amanda watched as a young father pulled his little boy on a sled past the house. In the kitchen, the oven buzzer sounded. Zuzu got up to take a pie from the oven.

Amanda turned to look at her. "I don't want the children to hear about this," she said.

"No," Zuzu agreed.

Chapter 55
3:30 p.m.

Mary was watching the news again, hoping to learn that the little girl who'd been crushed in the McClure building collapse had survived. And where was George? Mary had called his cell phone several times, but her grandson had not answered.

According to Fox News, the little girl, Gracie Bradshaw, was hanging on. Her brother had not been hurt as badly, but both his legs were broken. The children's mother was still in surgery.

What would happen to George if any of them died? Mary wondered. She suddenly wished her husband were still alive. He always knew what to do. She glanced up at the framed, yellowing drawing she had made not long after George had walked her home from the 1928 high school graduation dance. "George Lassos the Moon," she'd written beneath the image of an annoyed-looking moon with a lasso around it.

It had been nearly eighty years since that night – the first time George had showed any interest in her – and eighteen years since her beloved husband had died peacefully in his sleep, a brochure about cycling through China on his bedside table.

Mary turned off the television and lay back. She heard the sounds of Zuzu and Amanda preparing dinner. Other family members would join them later. They would all come in to visit her, and ask her how she felt. Well, she felt terrible, but the pneumonia had little to do with that.

Mary had been praying for George since she had heard the news about the building collapse, but now it was time to storm the gates of Heaven. Mary closed her eyes. "Dear Lord, please be with my grandson George. He needs your help so badly. Help him to see things as You see them..."

Would help arrive the way it had all those years ago, when Uncle Billy had lost that money, and Mary's beloved husband had considered throwing himself off the bridge?

Help had come then in the form of neighbors bringing money to make up the loss. They'd done it because they all loved Mary Bailey's husband. But nobody liked Mary's grandson, the man who thought he was too good for Bedford Falls. They certainly wouldn't go out of their way to help him.

But Mary loved him. So she continued to pray, long and hard, for George Bailey.

Chapter 56
3:32 p.m.

George paced his duplex, his hands jammed in his pockets, his emotions churning. What was he going to do? He suddenly remembered that he was supposed to be headed for Vermont. He could hardly go off skiing now; it would look so heartless. He turned his phone on in order to text the De Lucas. Whether they were annoyed or not now seemed of little importance.

He considered visiting the hospital where Tamera Bradshaw and her children were receiving treatment, then dismissed the idea. Reporters would be hanging out there, trying to interview Mr. Bradshaw, and besides, he thought, how would he feel if his own kids were in there, and the man responsible – the man the world *believed* was responsible, George amended hastily – showed up with flowers?

He'd punch him in the face.

George went to the kitchen to find something to eat. He found the remains of a chocolate pecan pie Amanda had baked before she left. He'd have that.

As he bit into it, George thought of his grandmother. She used to make him pies like this. He knew Amanda had obtained the recipe from her.

George suddenly longed for his grandmother. Was she dying, he wondered, thinking of Zuzu's email. And strangely enough, George longed for Bedford Falls. Amanda and the kids were there; he needed to patch things up with them, if he still could. All the aunts and uncles and cousins would be there, celebrating Christmas, listening to Aunt Janie play hymns in church. Later, in the firelit living room, filled with Grandfather's books, photographs, and mementos from his many trips, one of them would read aloud the little book Grandfather had written just for the family, about what had happened to him on Christmas Eve, 1945.

The reporters would not think of looking for him there. George would have a few days to recover from his life shattering to pieces all around him, and figure out what to do next.

His mind made up, George put on his overcoat, picked up the suitcase he'd already packed for Vermont, grabbed his keys, and took the elevator down to the garage. He'd turned his phone on again to check on calls, and forgotten to turn it back off. It rang again as George climbed into his Mercedes SUV – the only vehicle he owned that would make it through the snowy roads of upstate New York. He checked the number to make sure it wasn't Amanda, and turned it off again.

Chapter 57
3:45 p.m.

Cody Hepner turned his snowplow into the parking lot of the Bedford Falls Hospital. He'd been clearing streets since early morning, and was now clearing parking lots of essential services. The first area to clear was the hospital's heliport.

He'd been working continuously at this at least twelve hours a day for the past week. Since today was Christmas Eve, the town would be paying him double time. That was good, Cody thought, thinking of the Christmas bills that would arrive in January.

At that moment, he heard a grinding noise coming from his truck's transmission. The snowplow stopped dead in the middle of the heliport, and, despite everything Cody tried, would not start up again. Cody muttered darkly under his breath, got out of the truck, and went to call his boss.

Chapter 58
4:19 p.m.

As the winter darkness began to envelop him, George Bailey drove his Mercedes SUV skillfully up Interstate 80 West. An hour out of the city, the rain turned to snow, and the roads became slick. As he drove, he wondered if the police were looking for him, wanting answers to what had happened to the McClure Building. Well, they could wait until after Christmas, he thought.

Cars with loads of snow on top swished by him. For the first time since his parents had died, George was truly frightened. He would be blamed for the collapse of the McClure Building. If that little girl died, the press would blame him for that, too, just as they'd blamed him when that old woman committed suicide rather than leave her apartment in the Trent Towers. Amanda certainly blamed him. Why couldn't she understand that none of it was his responsibility? The contractor on the McClure building must have cut corners. Yes, he'd told him to make the deadline, but he certainly hadn't told him to do anything illegal.

He knew lawsuits would likely be filed. Would he lose everything he's spent the last eighteen years building? Would he face prison for putting people's lives in danger through his decision to use a contractor with a less-than-stellar reputation? Would Amanda make good on her threat to leave him?

Despite the warmth of the car, George shivered. *You were at fault*, a voice in his head told him as the highway lights flashed by him. *Everything that happened was your fault. And you deserve everything that's coming to you.*

Chapter 59
4:30 p.m.

At Mary Bailey's house, joyful chaos reigned.

Each member of the Bailey family had gone to visit Mary for at least a few minutes over the last two days. Now, they were involved in a mammoth gift-wrapping and cookie-eating session, catching up on each others' lives and teasing one another. The carpet was littered with cookie crumbs, bits of ribbon and fragments of wrapping paper, but, Zuzu thought, that didn't matter.

Zuzu looked with pleasure at her own two daughters, Lily and Rose, and their broods. Over by the fireplace sat Janie, her finger holding the ribbon knot on the package her granddaughter Kirsten was arranging. Zuzu knew it was a new bird feeder for Mary, to replace the one that had been blown down and broken during a storm.

Kirsten's older sister, Olivia, who took gift selections seriously, was intently wrapping a book for her grandfather Roberto about great restaurants in Northern Italy. Janie's granddaughter Bailey, her wrapping finished, was playing with Snickers, the latest of a long line of dachshunds Mary had adopted over the years. Zuzu had never understood her mother's passion for this breed. To Zuzu, dachshunds appeared to have been put together with spare parts.

Janie's son Eduardo was busy at the restaurant – a lot of people picked up takeout food on Christmas Eve, especially Roberto's special pizza – but Ed's wife and children were there, sitting before the fire on the worn red Oriental carpet. Tyler was reading on the faded old chintz-covered sofa; he would probably wrap his gifts at the last possible minute on Christmas morning. Sara and Isabella were playing together near the big

Christmas Tree, and Sophia was feeding Caitlin in the kitchen.

The younger children had already been put into their pajamas in anticipation of the fact that they were likely to fall asleep amidst the rubble, and would have to be carried upstairs to their beds. It was all part of Christmas.

The Hatch children and grandchildren were there, too, of course, although they were not staying in Mary's house. How amazing that they were all there – all except Janie's twins, Alex and Lonnie, who would be there for New Year's. How wonderful that they all wanted to come back to Bedford Falls every year or two for Christmas.

Everyone, that is, except George.

Zuzu watched Amanda as she set the big dining room table, first putting in the leaves, then adding the big white damask cloth, and then the lovely Haviland bone china plates Mary had bought in Paris in 1946. Waterford crystal goblets followed, and then Amanda carefully situated the two Waterford vases full of white Christmas roses, which Zuzu had arranged earlier in the day.

Setting the table for so many Baileys was a big job. The children would be fed first – the older ones at the dining room table, the younger ones in the kitchen. And then new plates and silverware would be laid for the adults.

A buffet dinner would really make more sense, Zuzu reflected, given the large number of Baileys and Hatches who were dining there tonight, but Mary had always delighted in having her family seated around her at the table – she at one end, and her husband at the other. So even though Mary would not be taking part in that evening's festivities, Zuzu honored her wishes.

"Wow, look at it snow!" yelled twelve-year-old Andrew Bailey. The younger children ran over to the big front window. Outside, the gentle snowfall had become more aggressive, delighting the great-grandchildren who lived in California.

"I hope it stops before we have to leave for church," Andrew's mother, Karen, said.

Zuzu realized she'd better check on Mary. She got up stiffly, her knees cracking, and walked down the hall to Mary's bedroom, where she put her ear to the door. She could hear nothing. But quietly opening the door, Zuzu found Mary awake. Her eyes were closed, and her hands were folded. Her lips were moving in prayer, her forehead wrinkled in concentration.

Zuzu closed the door. She could guess what Mary was praying about so intently on Christmas Eve.

Chapter 60
7:01 p.m.

The predicted blizzard struck just after seven o'clock. The wind yanked the front door of Martini's Place out of the hands of startled diners, who immediately scurried inside. Two blocks away, Jagan Chaudhury, taking an order from a customer for curried beef and rice, looked up in alarm as the wind roared down the street and rattled his windows.

At Gower Drugs, Travis Gower watched the weather forecast on a small television set he kept behind the counter. The prediction was that the blizzard would last several hours.

Travis's daughter was taking part in the Christmas Eve service at the Presbyterian Church. But now he wondered how they would get from their home on Chestnut Street to the church, situated near the center of town. Would the snowplows have time to clear the streets again in time for the 11 p.m. service?

Chapter 61
8:50 p.m.

Tommy Bailey knew he had had too much to drink, and he knew he was expected at home. But he was depressed. Christmas, a family holiday, always sent his spirits plunging into the cellar. He missed his father more this time of year, and felt more keenly his lack of a family of his own. His nieces and nephews, who had once liked to sit on his lap and listen to him sing, had grown up and had families of their own. Tommy had just turned sixty-six, and what did he have to show for it?

Tommy had gone to Martini's Place first, because he liked the atmosphere there better than anywhere else, but Roberto had gently but firmly cut him off after just two drinks. No matter. He'd walked down to the Kingfish Tavern and ordered several more.

Outside, darkness fell. Despite the blizzard, stores were open late for the last few sales, the sounds of Christmas carols emerging into the streets every time someone opened a door.

Tommy stumbled out of the Kingfish onto the sidewalk. What was he going to do next? Tommy thought hard. He was supposed to do something this evening. Oh, yes, it was Christmas Eve. Time to go home for the gathering of the clan.

Tommy stood in the wind and concentrated mightily, trying to remember where he'd left his car. Oh, yes, it was parked on front of Dillards, where's he'd been doing his last-minute Christmas shopping that afternoon. He never had much spending money, and hoped the families would enjoy the big tins of flavored popcorn he'd purchased.

Tommy walked the block to Dillards, pulled out his keys, and managed to unlock the car. Pulling open the door, he half-fell, half sat in the driver's seat. Shutting the door with some difficulty, Tommy put the key in the ignition.

Chapter 62
8:50 p.m.

In the living room of the Bailey house, Marianne sat by herself in a rocking chair, her arms wound tightly around herself, watching her cousins wrap gifts to the blare of *How the Grinch Stole Christmas* on the television. Dinner was over, and several of the aunts and great-aunts were in the kitchen, packing away leftover turkey for Christmas Day, and carefully hand-washing Mary's china, silver, and crystal.

Amanda dried her hands on a towel and wandered back into the living room. Observing the sad expression on her daughter's face, she picked her up and sat down in the rocker herself, Marianne in her lap.

"Is anything wrong, Sugarplum?" she asked.

Marianne's face crumpled.

"Daddy's not here," she said, pressing her face against her mother's neck. "Everybody else's daddy is here."

Amanda hugged her, trying to think of something that would cheer up the little girl.

Observing them, Zuzu said, "Marianne, I have to take some Christmas cookies over to the Lins' house across the street. Will you be a love and come with me?"

Zuzu had planned to take the cookies over the next morning, when the weather was better, but never mind. Blizzard or no blizzard, Marianne needed a distraction. And it was only just across the street. Marianne wiped her eyes with the backs of her hands.

"Okay," she said, her voice wavering a bit.

Amanda bundled her up in her pink coat, hat, gloves, and boots. The blizzard was still going strong, with snow flying into the faces of all who dared to go out. Amanda began to have second thoughts about Marianne leaving the house.

"I'm not so sure this is a good idea," she ventured.

"It'll be fun!" Zuzu robustly insisted, zipping up her own coat and wrapping a blue scarf around her neck.

Amanda reluctantly smiled. She knew Zuzu didn't really want to go out in the storm, but she would do almost anything to cheer up a child.

Holding the plate of cookies in one hand, Zuzu pulled open the front door with the other, then grabbed Marianne's hand.

"Let's go, sweetie," she said.

Chapter 63
8:55 p.m.

Tommy turned on his windshield wipers and pulled out onto Genesee Street. He knew he shouldn't be driving in this insane weather, but he needed to get home. He carefully drove a few blocks and then turned into Red Oak Street. *Whoops*, he thought. *Wrong road*. He managed to turn around, illegally, and headed back to the last intersection. He squinted, trying to read the street signs in the dark. Sycamore Street was just ahead. He carefully turned onto it, and heaved a sigh of relief.

Tommy drove slowly and carefully down Sycamore Street in an effort to keep his car in the correct lane. It was so hard to see with all that snow flying around. And the heat of his car was making him sleepy. He slowed almost to a crawl.

Behind him, someone honked impatiently. Tommy peered into the rearview mirror. It was Ralph Bishop. Bishop was always in a hurry, Tommy thought irritably.

"So you think I'm going too slow, huh, buddy?" he said aloud. He put his foot down on the gas.

Chapter 64
8:55 p.m.

Just as Zuzu was closing the door behind them, Snickers raced outside.

"Oh, no! We've got to get her back inside," Zuzu said.

But Snickers – who'd been kept inside far too much in the last few days – had other ideas. Spotting a squirrel, she raced after it, barking madly.

"I'll get her!" Marianne shouted, running after the little dog.

Zuzu was never to forget what happened next.

Snickers ran into the street after the squirrel. Marianne ran after Snickers. And a car traveling slowly down Sycamore Street suddenly sped up, striking Marianne. The little girl's body flew into the air, slammed against a tree, and then fell to the ground. Bright drops of blood began dripping on the snow from her head.

Chapter 65
9:15 p.m.

In the Bedford Falls Hospital emergency room, nurse Sara Hernandez hooked up a drip to the unconscious little girl while another nurse quickly cut off Marianne's clothing. The child was soaked in her own blood, most of it coming from her head. Doctors and nurses swarmed over her, looking for broken bones, and quickly checking her pulse, temperature, and respiration. Nurse Katie White pulled back Marianne's eyelid to check for pupil dilation, and then checked for blood coming out of her ears.

"We need X-rays and an EKG," ordered Dr. Albert Lin, who had been unlucky enough to draw Christmas Eve duty that year. Minutes later, he knew the extent of Marianne's injuries. Her spleen would have to be removed. The head injury was even more serious. She needed a neurosurgeon, and Bedford Falls Hospital didn't have one.

Cases like this were rare in Bedford Falls, but when they did occur, patients were usually stabilized and taken by ambulance or helicopter to St. Elizabeth's Hospital in Rochester, where they were equipped to deal with such severe injuries. But the blizzard had made both road travel and helicopter flights impossible.

How were they going to get the little girl to Rochester? Dr. Lin asked himself. Mary Bailey was his across-the-street neighbor; this was her great-granddaughter. They simply had to save her.

Chapter 66
9:20 p.m.

Outside the emergency room door, Amanda Bailey sat trembling. Aunt Zuzu had not wanted to leave Mary, and the older children had stayed behind to look after the younger ones, but Aunt Janie and most of the rest of the adult Baileys were there. Many of them didn't know Amanda very well, but family was family.

The door to the emergency room swung open and Dr. Lin emerged. Amanda leaped to her feet.

"She's alive," Dr. Lin told her. "But she needs immediate surgery. With your permission, I'm going to remove her spleen. We can't wait on this."

Amanda swayed, and Dr. Lin caught her. "Better sit down," he said gently.

Amanda sat down, and Janie took her hand.

"I'm afraid she also has a cerebral hematoma, which means her brain is bleeding and swelling from hitting that tree so hard," he went on. "She needs to have a piece of her skull removed to relieve the pressure. We don't have anybody here who's had any experience doing that. She needs a neurosurgeon, and we don't have one here. St. Elizabeth's Medical Center in Rochester has one."

Dr. Lin sat down next to Amanda and lowered his voice for the worst news. "The problem is, Mrs. Bailey, we can't get her to Rochester in this weather. It's fifty miles to St. Elizabeth's, and I'm told there's no way of driving there in this blizzard. And a helicopter won't be able to make it, either – at least, not until the blizzard ends."

Amanda's face went white.

"We're going to start on the splenectomy right away," Dr. Lin said gently. "We need you to sign some papers."

Chapter 67
10 p.m.

As abruptly as it had begun, the blizzard ended. The wind stopped, and after seven straight days of snow, the air was eerily empty of flakes, and silent.

The blizzard had dumped an additional eighteen inches of snow on Bedford Falls. The city's snowplows were immediately dispatched in an effort to clear the streets again for last-minute shoppers and the various Christmas Eve services that evening. Many stores made a high percentage of their annual gross income on Christmas Eve, and often stayed open until 11 p.m. As well, two of the town's churches began their Christmas Eve services at that hour.

At the Bedford Falls Presbyterian church, the church sexton, Todd Macklin, was on the phone with a parishioner, a farmer who might be cajoled into coming into town early to clear the church parking lot with his snowplow; there was no way the town would get around to it before the 11 p.m. service began. But as they spoke, Macklin heard a terrific cracking noise outside. He ran to a window in time to see the huge old oak tree, planted a hundred years ago when the church was built, topple under the weight of the snow. It crashed down in front of the entrance to the parking lot.

Chapter 68
10:15 p.m.

Between rush-hour traffic and bad weather, it took George Bailey six-and-a-half hours before he reached the exit that would take him winding down Mt. Bedford into Bedford Falls. He slowly made his way down to the bridge, just half a mile above the center of town.

Looming up before him in the darkness was the sign reading, "You are now in Bedford Falls." The city fathers had put one up before every entrance into town. George had heard on the radio about the blizzard that had struck Bedford Falls that evening. But luckily, the storm had ended a few minutes ago, and now, just a few exhausted flakes fluttered down on Mt. Bedford.

Biggest drifts I've ever seen here, George thought as he began crossing the bridge. Suddenly, George's headlights picked out the figure of a deer – or was it a man? – on the bridge just yards ahead. Horrified, George slammed on the brakes and swerved. His car spun out of control and slammed into the iron railing of the bridge.

Stunned, George sat for a few moments, mentally checking himself over for pain. He'd thrown his hands up when he'd realized he was going to crash, and the ring on his right hand had struck his forehead, gashing it badly. Blood dripped from the cut onto his expensive cashmere coat.

George cursed softly but violently as he pushed aside the inflated airbag and climbed out of the warmth of his SUV into the cold darkness. His shoes and trouser cuffs instantly soaked up the cold slush on the bridge that sat beneath the new snow. Snowflakes swirled around him, mixing with puffs of his breath. In the silence, George heard the sound of the Bedford River rushing away below him. He'd walked across this bridge with his grandfather countless times as a boy, fishing pole in hand.

George carefully stepped through the slush to survey the damage to the car. The hood was badly dented and a headlight was smashed. The other light illuminated the pine trees that bordered the river. Glancing around him, George saw no sign of whoever or whatever it was that he thought he'd seen. That meant it had to have been a deer, George thought.

He suddenly felt nausea rise up, and grabbed the railing to keep his balance. He forced himself to wait a few more moments to recover from the shock and dizziness. Shivering, he pulled a handkerchief out of his pocket and gingerly pressed it to his forehead. He glanced back at the car hoping it was still drivable.

The breeze picked up, spinning the snowflakes in mad circles. It was a cold, whispering breeze, which seemed to be trying to tell him something. The SUV's second headlight abruptly went out, leaving George in almost total darkness. He shivered again, not from cold, this time, but from a sense of being utterly alone in the world – a frozen world in which time itself seemed to have stopped.

George took a few steps off the bridge so he could look down on the town below. It was lit up with Christmas lights. He could see the Presbyterian Church steeple, and, although he could not make it out, he knew the Bailey Brothers Building and Loan was down there, too, and his grandmother's house. And Amanda.

His head throbbed, but it was time to get moving.

George turned and walked back to the SUV. As he put his hand on the door handle, George felt the blast of a sudden gust of wind. And then, footsteps crunching in the snow behind him.

He spun around. The footsteps came to a halt. Standing just a few feet away was a short, plump, elderly man wearing an old-fashioned suit, a polka-dotted bow tie, a fedora, and – astonishingly – what appeared to be a fine set of wings. His kindly face broke into a smile.

"Hello, George," the man said.

Chapter 69
10:15 p.m.

"Dr. Lin."

An intern stuck his head in the door of the operating room, where Dr. Lin was stitching up Marianne.

"What is it?" Dr. Lin asked.

"The good news is, the weather has improved and they can get a helicopter here now," the intern said.

"And the bad news?"

"I just found out that a snowplow stopped dead on the heliport," the intern told him. "Which means – "

"We can't land a bird there," Dr. Lin finished for him.

"That's right."

The two doctors looked at each other bleakly.

"Sorry, Dr. Lin."

Chapter 70
10:16 p.m.

"I hope," the little man said, "that you aren't going to make me jump into the river, like your grandfather did."

He smiled, his old eyes crinkling merrily.

George put his hand to his forehead again. He must have lost more blood than he thought.

"Did I hit you?" he asked the stranger.

"No, I'm fine, George."

"How do you know my name?"

"I'm your guardian angel."

"Oh, please," George said irritably. Of all the people in Bedford Falls, he had to run into this drunken old fool.

"I AM your guardian angel!"

"Look, I don't have time for this. My grandmother may be dying and —"

"I know. And you haven't seen her for quite a while, have you?" the man said sympathetically.

George sighed in irritation and looked at his watch. He wanted badly to get to his grandmother's house, but he couldn't leave this nutty old man out here on the bridge. He'd freeze to death.

"Do you want a ride?" he asked brusquely as he pulled open his car door.

The little man laughed. "I don't think your car can take me to the place I live."

"Well, I can take you to the police station, anyway. Get in."

"Sure, George. I've never ridden in an SUV. Come to think of it, I haven't ridden in anything but a coach – "

"Just shut up and get in."

"All right, all right."

George started up the SUV. It seemed to be running okay, he thought. If only his head would stop throbbing. He was just a short drive from the Bailey house. But first he had to dump this old geezer at the police station.

"What's your name," he asked the old man.

"I'm Clarence Oddbody."

Clarence Oddbody. Memories of his grandfather's Christmas storytelling swam to the surface. Clarence... Grandfather's angel.

Well, this crazy old guy must have heard the story and decided to play the role. George had read of people doing things like this. Some unknown person took roses and cognac to the Baltimore grave of Edgar Allen Poe every year on the anniversary of his death. And there were those who, on the anniversary of the *Titanic* sinking, dressed up in Edwardian clothing and dined on the same foods the passengers had enjoyed just before the ship struck an iceberg. People with nothing better to do dressed up as Elvis. And this old guy must have somehow gotten hold of a copy of Grandfather's little book about his Christmas Eve adventures in 1945 and decided to act out the role of Clarence, complete with the wings he'd supposedly earned showing Grandfather that he'd really lived a wonderful life.

Well, George wasn't going to play along. But it was strange that the old man knew his name. Wait – he must have been waiting for Grandfather to show up – or someone who planned to play Grandfather.

"You look like him," Clarence said.

"Like who?"

"Like your grandfather."

This guy must have really done his research, George thought. He might have gotten hold of pictures of the whole family.

"Yes, I do look a lot like my grandfather," he replied coolly.

"What a pity you don't act more like him," Clarence said softly. "If you were more like him, that little girl in New York wouldn't be hanging between life and death right now. Your son wouldn't have gotten into trouble with the police, throwing rocks at that building..."

This guy obviously reads the New York papers and watched that afternoon's broadcasts, George thought, anger rising up in his chest at the old man's audacity.

"... And your wife would not be seriously thinking of leaving you."

George slammed on the brakes and the SUV swiveled in a half-circle before coming to a stop.

"How did you know that?" he shouted.

"I know all about you," Clarence replied with a smile. "I've known you since you were a little boy, sitting on your grandfather's knee while he told you stories. You used to love playing with that little replica of the Building and Loan."

Clarence held his feet towards the SUV's heater, enjoying the warmth.

"Remember how you used to take pennies out of your grandfather's pocket for your bank? Your cousins always returned the pennies when they were finished playing with the toy. But you always kept them. And you always took more than your share of your grandmother's cookies. These were small faults, but your grandparents worried that they would turn into big ones."

George's heart was thudding in his chest.

"Obviously, you must be a friend of my family to know all the family gossip, including gossip about my wife and me."

"The only member of your family I ever met was your grandfather, George," Clarence replied.

George rolled his eyes, sighed in annoyance, and pressed the gas pedal again. He was now about to enter the little town's commercial district, lit up with Christmas lights and wreaths.

"I suppose," George said sarcastically, as the damaged SUV rolled down Genesee street, "that this is where you tell me I've really lived a wonderful life."

"No, George," Clarence said soberly. "I came down to tell you that you've lived a terrible life."

Chapter 71
10:17 p.m.

Amanda, Janie, and the other Baileys prayed desperately for Marianne in the hospital chapel. Dr. Lin had said the splenectomy would take forty-five minutes to an hour, depending on whether he found damage to any other organs that would need repairing. Nearly an hour had passed, and they were still waiting for news.

Amanda had called George's cell phone repeatedly, and texted him as well, but he had evidently turned off his phone. She had also tried his office, only to be told he had left that morning for the company brunch at the Plaza, and not come back. Nor did he answer their home phone. *Where is he?* Amanda thought.

The door to the chapel opened, and Dr. Lin put his head in.

"Mrs. Bailey?"

Amanda turned around and then jumped up.

"How is she?" she asked.

"She's holding her own," Dr. Lin replied.

Why do doctors always say things like that? Amanda wondered. *It doesn't really mean anything, except that she's still alive.*

"The problem is, we still need to deal with her brain swelling."

"You said we couldn't helicopter Marianne to Rochester until the weather improved. The blizzard stopped a few minutes ago. Does that mean they can come pick up Marianne?"

Dr. Lin looked at her grimly. "They can – but there's a problem. A snowplow stopped dead in the middle of the heliport. I'm told there's no way a bird can land there."

"Then what are we going to do?" Amanda cried.

Chapter 72
10:22 p.m.

"I've done no such thing," George told Clarence irritably. "I've had a great life. I founded my own business. I build big buildings and remodel others. I'm a very rich man. I just gave ten million dollars to an art museum to buy a Picasso. And I have a beautiful wife and two healthy kids."

"I notice you place your family last on your list of accomplishments," Clarence observed as George carefully negotiated the SUV along Genesee Street, slick and narrowed by the piles of snow.

"That doesn't mean anything."

"Oh, I think it does. It means that you put your business and your money ahead of them."

"Nonsense."

"Well, we'll drop the subject for now. By the way, this vehicle is very comfortable. And so warm on such a cold night."

"It should be. It cost enough."

"George, do you know why I'm here?"

"You just told me. You want to tell me why I've lived such a terrible life."

"I'm here, George, because your grandmother has been praying for you all afternoon."

George, approaching the north end of Genesee Street, sighed. Only a few minutes longer and this nutter would be the problem of the police.

"If you say so, Clarence."

"You still don't believe me, do you? Neither did your grandfather."

Clarence chuckled. "You have no idea how much trouble I had convincing him that I really was an angel."

"Oh, yes, I do. He wrote a little book about it. You were the star."

"Oh, my," Clarence laughed delightedly. "I had no idea. Do you have a copy of it? If you do, I'd like – "

A disapproving rumble came from the heavens.

"Okay, okay," Clarence muttered.

"Sounds like we're going to have another storm," George said. He slid the car into a parking space next to the police station.

"Here we are."

"But George, I haven't finished yet. I still haven't told you – "

"I'm in a hurry," George cut him off. "My grandmother isn't doing well. She may be dying. So please – just get out. Someone at the police station will help you."

Clarence thought furiously for a few seconds. It had worked before, he thought to himself. It might just work again...

"Hey." George tapped Clarence's shoulder. "Time to go."

It's time to go, all right, Clarence thought. He shut his eyes tight and focused.

The car's engine suddenly cut out. The heater turned off; so did the headlights.

"What the – " George turned the ignition switch. Nothing. He pressed the gas pedal several times, and tried again. Still nothing.

George swore savagely.

"It's no use, George."

With an effort, George controlled his temper. He'd endured a horrible shock that afternoon when the top floor of his building had collapsed, badly injuring a family, followed by a long drive from New York to Bedford Falls. He'd damaged his car and his head throbbed. He was hungry, and he was anxious about Mary. And now this strange little man, this *reenactor* of the Bailey family myth, was the frosting on the cake.

"You see, George, I'm the one who shut down your car. And I'm the only one who can start it again."

George could stand it no longer. He threw open his door, got out into the cold night air, and bent to glare into Clarence's face, lit by the light of one of Bedford Falls's old-fashioned orb lights.

"Get out!" George snarled.

"Sure, George," Clarence said. "But you're going with me."

"I'm not going anywhere except – "

"We have a lot further to go than your grandfather did," Clarence noted as he climbed out of the car. "Good thing I have my wings."

He reached out and grabbed George's arm.

"Hang on!"

George angrily tried to shake off Clarence's hands, but the little man had a surprisingly strong grip. Just then, a tremendous wind rose up out of nowhere, and swirled around the two. George could no longer see anything but Clarence. Suddenly frightened, he shouted, "What's going on?"

"First, we're going to New York," Clarence said.

Chapter 73
10:22 p.m.

"I want to see her," Amanda said.

Dr. Lin led her to the hospital's Intensive Care Unit. Amanda was horrified by what she saw. The little girl was still unconscious, her small body hooked up to machines. Her face was bruised and swelling a bit from hitting the ground after the collision with the tree. A drip was instilling medications to slow the swelling of her brain.

What they needed was a miracle. Tears sliding down her face, Amanda took Marianne's small hand into hers and began to pray.

Chapter 74
10:25 p.m.

The rush of wind lashing George and Clarence lasted only moments. When it stopped, George nearly fell over. Clarence tightened his grip on his arm.

"Easy there, George."

The first thing George noticed was that the lights on the stores were much brighter, and that the stores themselves were much bigger. He realized he was no longer standing on a quiet street in Bedford Falls. Swarms of people rushed by him, carrying packages.

Stunned and frightened, George discovered that he was, indeed, in the heart of Manhattan. His car was gone. But Clarence was still there, looking intently into George's face. He smiled gently.

"Do you believe me now?"

George rubbed his hand over his face, and reached down to pinch his arm. He wasn't dreaming. He wasn't drunk. He wasn't dead. Which meant that...

Clarence really was an angel.

George swallowed hard, and sought to regain control of this unbelievable situation.

"Why did you bring me to New York?"

"I wanted you to see Amanda," Clarence replied.

"But she's in Bedford Falls, with my grandmother and the kids."

"No, she isn't," Clarence responded. "Like your grandfather, you're being given a great gift: A chance to see what the world would have been like without you."

George thought swiftly, remembering some of the details of his grandfather's story.

"Which means... I'm not married to Amanda. She's a librarian."

"You're half right," Clarence replied. "You're not married to Amanda. But she's not a librarian. She's married to somebody else."

Chapter 75
10:26 p.m.

George and Clarence walked a block south. They were nowhere near the neighborhood in which George lived, but having built or rebuilt so many buildings, George was able to tell at a glance what the brownstones in this neighborhood went for. They were worth far less than his own duplex penthouse. Clarence stopped before the door of one that George estimated would sell for about $800,000.

"Now what?" George asked.

"Now, we wait," Clarence said.

"What are we waiting for?" he asked.

His answer was the sound of laughter. Amanda's laughter. She suddenly came around the corner of the building with a handsome, dark-haired man. They were holding hands, and the man abruptly bent down to kiss Amanda. At the sight, George felt a piercing pain shoot through his chest.

Amanda was dressed simply in jeans, a thick turtleneck sweater, boots, and a Burberry coat, a far cry from the designer clothes, furs, and jewels she wore when she was out with George. She was talking animatedly to the man she was with.

"Who is that guy?" George asked.

"He's Doctor Joshua Purdue – Amanda's husband. His specialty is pediatric surgery," Clarence answered. "He and Amanda are returning home from a spaghetti dinner with friends who support his work on a Mercy Ship. Dr. Purdue spends a few weeks every year traveling to ports in Africa, performing surgeries free of charge on children with devastating birth defects."

"Does Amanda go with him?"

"No," Clarence replied. "She stays home with their five children."

"Five?!"

"Why are you so surprised, George? You've always known Amanda wanted a big family."

George did know, but it sank in now, for the first time, just how badly Amanda wanted more babies. He'd thought two children were plenty. With a different husband, she had had three more. A mixture of anger, jealousy, hurt, and shame drove him to tell Clarence, "He can't make much money giving away his time like that."

"He doesn't care about having a big income, and neither does Amanda," Clarence told him. "They care about helping poor children lead better lives."

Purdue and Amanda climbed the steps to their front door, unlocked it, and went inside. Clarence and George walked down the sidewalk slowly enough that George could take a long look in the front window. He saw several children in pajamas race to their parents and fling themselves gleefully into their arms. One of them looked a lot like Peter, George thought. His chest tightened as he watched the boy, who must have been around eleven years old, embrace his father and drag him off by the hand. George tried to remember the last time Peter had hugged him.

He couldn't.

A young woman, probably the babysitter, brought a baby to Amanda for a goodnight kiss. Amanda lifted the infant above her head, making the child laugh, and then brought its little face down for repeated kisses.

Amanda looked so happy. George's heart twisted. He tried to remember the last time she had looked this happy with him.

He couldn't.

"It's kind of hard watching that, isn't it?" Clarence said sympathetically. "Hard to see how much happier your wife would have been if she had never met you."

George couldn't speak.

Amanda and her husband were now leading their children to bed. When George and Clarence could no longer see them, Clarence took George's arm again.

"Now we're going to pay a visit to another family," he said.

"Which family?" George asked, surprised. But his words were torn away by the sudden wind that swirled around them.

Chapter 76
10:26 p.m.

As the people of Bedford Falls learned of Marianne's accident, they began arriving at the hospital. Each newcomer learned how severe the little girl's injuries were, and of the need to get her to St. Elizabeth's trauma center in Rochester. Many of them went to the hospital's chapel to pray. So did several of the off-duty doctors and nurses. Nobody could bear the thought that Mary Bailey's great-granddaughter might die on Christmas Eve. Nobody had told Mary what had happened, fearing the effect on her already precarious health.

"Please, God, don't take this little girl," prayed Kate O'Brien. "Please help us find a way to save her."

"Jesus, Joseph and Mary," whispered Gabriela Martini, "please save this dear child. Please help us find a way for us to take her to St. Elizabeth's."

Jagan Chaudhari, who had immediately left his restaurant when he heard the news, was on his knees in the chapel, tears running down his face. "Lord, this is George Bailey's great-granddaughter. Please don't take her yet. She has her whole life ahead of her."

"Lord, we need a miracle," prayed Dr. Baldwin, his head bowed, his hands clasped between his knees. "You know what Marianne needs. Please help us find a way."

In the back of the chapel, a man quietly entered and sat on the back pew. It was Tommy. He put his head in his hands and began to weep.

Chapter 77
10:36 p.m.

The swirling wind stopped abruptly. George recognized the building as one of his own: Trent Towers.

"What are we doing here?" he asked.

"We're going to visit a lady named Agnes Hubbard. She lives here."

George felt a chill. "Isn't she the woman who – ?"

"Yes," Clarence replied. "She's the woman who killed herself rather than leave the only home she'd known for sixty-four years."

"I suppose you're going to blame me for that," George said sourly.

"No," Clarence replied. "Remember, George, I came down here simply to show you what would have happened if you'd never been born."

The two entered the building and Clarence pushed the elevator button. George felt a sense of alarm.

"Clarence," he said, "I don't want to see this woman, and she sure doesn't want to see me."

"You're forgetting, she won't know who you are."

They boarded the elevator, which lifted them to the third floor. The doors opened, and George looked down the hall. Funny, the hallway looked a lot nicer than he remembered. Somebody must have fixed the place up.

Music floated down the hall from apartment 324. Clarence knocked. Moments later, the door was yanked open by an attractive young brunette with a bright red drink in her hand.

"Come in!" she invited with a grin. "We're all getting sloshed."

Clarence eagerly followed the girl into the apartment, noisy with loud music, louder conversation, and even louder laughter.

George reluctantly followed Clarence in. Somebody shoved a drink into his hand. People of all ages surrounded the piano, where a young man played "The Twelve Days of Christmas" as rapidly as he could, until the singers fell behind and collapsed with laughter.

"Are you a friend of Grandma's?" asked the young woman who'd opened the door to them.

Startled, George replied, "No."

"You're a relative, then?"

"No."

The girl cocked her head to one side and gave George a curious half-smile. "Well... what are you doing here, then? Oh, wait: You're a neighbor and the noise is bothering you."

"No, I'm not a neighbor," George answered, beginning to feel embarrassed. The young woman seemed to find him amusing. He took a sip of the drink. Cranberry juice, grapefruit juice, vodka, and one or two other ingredients, he thought.

"Well, whoever you are, we're glad you're here." She pointed to a white-haired old woman sitting in a dark green armchair, a joyful smile on her face. "We decided to surprise Grandma and come home for Christmas this year. I live with my folks in Texas, and my brother just flew in from Saudi Arabia. Oh, I'm Frankie, by the way. Named for my grandpa. He's gone, though."

As the girl chattered on, George watched as Clarence grabbed a plate, filled it with cookies, and joined the group at the piano. They had just begun to sing "Deck the Halls." The angel, George noticed irrelevantly, had a fine tenor voice.

"Fa-la-la-la-la, la-la-la-la!" Clarence sang lustily. He bit into another cookie and wiped the crumbs from his mouth.

"Sugar cookies! I haven't had one of those for at least three hundred years!" The young people laughed.

"Your friend looks like a lot of fun," Frankie said. "Does he know Grandma?"

Clarence, overhearing Frankie's question, called back an answer: "I've known her for eighty-seven years!"

"You mean you've known her since she was a baby?" Frankie asked with a laugh.

"That's right!" Clarence responded cheerfully.

George looked again at Agnes. A deeply tanned man in late middle-age brought her a wrapped gift, handed it to her, and bent down to kiss her.

This is the woman who killed herself, George thought. *If she'd only waited –*

"You're forgetting, George. If you had never been born, somebody else would have owned this building."

Evidently Clarence could read his thoughts.

"Like you, that owner wanted to upgrade this building. But unlike you, he decided to let people like Agnes live out their lives in their apartments. She had no reason to want to kill herself."

"But all of these people – " George floundered. "Why didn't they come see her in her other life? She might not have killed herself if she'd known they were coming!"

"They did come to see her," Clarence answered quietly. George strained to hear his next words over the racket of the piano and a dozen relatives and friends of Agnes Hubbard singing and laughing. "They decided to surprise her. They arrived on the day she committed suicide. They attended her funeral, instead."

With Clarence's sorrowing eyes on him, George felt a sense of shame rise up in his chest – a sense of shame that had not visited him for many a year.

"Come on, George, we've been here long enough," Clarence said, stuffing a few cookies into his pocket. He took George's arm and the music began fading away. George's vision was blurred, and the world began to spin again.

"Where are we going this time?" he asked.

"You'll see," Clarence responded.

Chapter 78
10:40 p.m.

As Tommy Bailey wept quietly, he listened to all the prayers going up for his great-niece. Eighteen inches of fresh snow covered everything in Bedford Falls. He knew there was no way to get Marianne to St. Elizabeth's in Rochester. And there was no way they could land a helicopter on the hospital heliport. They needed a miracle. They needed...

Suddenly Tommy's head snapped up. He remembered one of the last jobs he had worked: helping pave the big new parking lot at Bedford Falls Presbyterian Church... the big, *flat* parking lot. A parking lot big enough to...

Tommy jumped up, raced out of the chapel, and ran down the stairs to the third floor to find Amanda. He spotted her as she emerged from Marianne's room and began addressing the throngs of people who had arrived to find out what was happening to Mary Bailey's great-granddaughter. Tommy ignored the hostile looks his neighbors gave him, and grabbed Amanda's arm.

"Amanda. We can use the Presbyterian Church parking lot!"

An exhausted Amanda stared at him, uncomprehending.

"The parking lot," Tommy repeated. "We can use it to land the helicopter. There's plenty of room!"

There was stunned silence for a few moments. Then, Dr. Baldwin spoke up.

"There's at least eighteen inches of snow on that parking lot – "

"And we can't get a snowplow on it," said Douglas Tucker, who was a deacon at the church. "A big tree came down at the entrance to the parking lot a little while ago – "

"We'll shovel it off!" Tommy said excitedly. "If we all get a shovel, it won't take more than half an hour!"

Dr. Lin's eyes lit up.

"I'll call the airport and let them know they'll have a place to land a bird in about forty-five minutes."

Chapter 79
10:46 p.m.

George shivered with cold. The rain had started up again. As the cars flashed by, headlights glowing and wipers rapidly swishing away the rain, George searched for a street sign.

"What are we doing on East 38th Street?" he asked. "I don't know anybody who lives here."

"Just wait a minute," Clarence said as he opened an umbrella.

"Where did that umbrella come from?"

"I have my wings, now," Clarence said smugly. "I can do lots of things you can't do."

Well, good for you, George thought. "I heard that, George," Clarence admonished him. "Remember, I'm an angel, first class. Now, pay attention. This is the family we've come to see."

The door of the building before them swung open. A man and a woman stepped out, followed by two young children, well bundled against the cold December air. The little boy held his arms up, and his father, as George supposed him to be, picked him up and pulled the child's back over his head. The family walked down the street.

Watching them, George said flatly, "I have no idea who those people are."

"They're the Bradshaw family. Does that name ring a bell?"

George felt a shock of recognition. Without thinking, he said, "But they live in the McClure Building! They don't live here, on East 38th Street!"

"Oh yes, they do. And do you know why they're living here?"

George shook his head.

"It's because their apartment in the McClure Building isn't finished yet. It won't be finished until February."

"But it was finished on December twenty-first!" George protested.

"YOU finished it on December twenty-first," Clarence reminded him. "You told the contractor to get the project done by that date, or else. You wanted the new tenants in their apartments by then, paying rent, so the contractor cut corners."

"But I didn't tell him to cut corners and put people's lives in danger."

Even as he spoke the words, George felt his guilt. He'd known perfectly well that he hadn't left the contractor any choice. And he'd known the contractor had been in trouble before with buildings that didn't – or shouldn't have – passed inspection.

"I'm glad you understand that," Clarence said softly, once again reading George's thoughts. "Let's see where the Bradshaws are going."

George and Clarence walked down the wet streets, traveling several blocks until they came to a church. They watched as the Bradshaws walked in. Clarence pulled on George's arm.

"Come on, we're going in, too."

The church was simply but beautifully decorated with white candles, pine cones, and pine branches. Seating himself in the back pew, George inhaled the fragrances of pine needles, candle wax, and old hymnbooks. The organist was softly playing Christmas hymns. George watched as families, dressed in their Christmas best, walked down the aisle to find their seats.

At the front of the church, he saw the little Bradshaw girl, standing with other members of the children's choir in front of the altar. At their feet were dozens of red poinsettias, donated by church members.

The minister, a balding, middle-aged man wearing a white robe with a purple stole, entered through a side door near the altar and beamed at the congregation.

"Merry Christmas!" he welcomed them.

"Merry Christmas, Pastor Andrews!" the congregation answered.

"We will now hear from our children's choir, which has been practicing for weeks for this very special program," Pastor Andrews announced. He sat down, and the choir director stood up. She led the children into their first hymn, "Go Tell It On the Mountain." When they finished the first verse, Gracie Bradshaw stepped forward for her solo.

"The shepherds feared and twembled, When lo! Above the earth, wang out the angel chorus, that hailed our Savior's birth," Gracie sang.

In the front pew, her parents watched with huge smiles on their faces. Mr. Bradshaw was discreetly filming his daughter.

Enjoying the peaceful scene, George began to relax. When was the last time he'd been in church? he wondered.

"About seven years ago, when Marianne was baptized," Clarence answered him.

George glared at Clarence. "Will you *please* stop doing that?"

"Sorry, George. Didn't mean to annoy you."

The children began their second hymn, "The First Noel," and George enjoyed hearing their sweet young voices raised in song. He realized he was more relaxed than he'd been since...

George frowned. He couldn't remember the last time he'd felt so at peace. The children finished their song, smiled shyly at their parents, and began singing "Joy to the World." In the pew just ahead of George, a baby gurgled in its mother's arms. She put it over her shoulder, and began rubbing its back.

"... Let ev'ry heart, prepare him room," the children warbled.

Peace. Beauty. Warmth. *I could stay here forever*, George thought.

Clarence broke in on his thoughts. "This," he said, "is what the Bradshaw family would have been doing tonight if you'd never been born. Instead, they're in the hospital. Mr. Bradshaw isn't watching his little girl sing; he's begging her doctors to save her life – that is, when he's not in the chapel praying. His wife is still in surgery. And his little boy has two broken legs. He may never be able to play soccer again, which he loves – or any other sport."

George put his hands to his face. How much worse was this going to get? he wondered in despair. Hadn't he done *anything* worthwhile in this world? Or had he been responsible for nothing but pain?

"Let's go," Clarence said, standing up. George stood, too, and followed Clarence outside into the rain.

"There's just one more family I want to show you," Clarence said, taking George's arm. "They live in Seneca Falls. We're going to revisit a decision you made when you were twenty."

George stumbled and nearly fell. A paralyzing fear shot through his body.

"Oh, no," he whispered. "Please, Clarence, no. I'm begging you."

Chapter 80
10:47 p.m.

Word traveled swiftly all over town as Bedford Fallsians called friends or ran to knock on dozens of doors: Mary Bailey's great-granddaughter needed to be flown to St. Elizabeth's trauma center, and a helicopter was arriving at 11:25 p.m. to take her there. In order for the 'copter to land, everyone needed to bring a shovel to the church parking lot and start shoveling snow as fast as they could.

Matthew Bailey Gruszecki ran straight from the hospital to the church, shoved open the front door, and shouted for Larry Partridge, the church sexton.

"We need to land a helicopter on the church parking lot to take my cousin to St. Elizabeth's Hospital in Rochester! Turn on all the lights!"

Partridge immediately flipped on the floodlights on the church building, illuminating the parking lot, and ran to grab two big shovels.

"Let's go!" he told Matthew.

The two ran outside and began shoveling the snow off the north end of the lot. It wasn't long before they had company.

On Beech Street, a desperate Zuzu pounded on a door decorated with a fresh pine wreath and tiny silver balls. A young, dark-haired woman answered the door.

"My little niece needs to go to a trauma center in Rochester!" Zuzu gasped. "We need to shovel the Presbyterian Church parking lot so the helicopter can land there! Please come and help us! Please bring a shovel."

In her panic, Zuzu had not recognized the young woman as Anna Cruz. But Anna Cruz remembered Zuzu; she was the lady who had talked the Building and Loan people into loaning them the money for their house. She turned to shout in Spanish to the people seated around a big dining room table. The entire Cruz family – around twenty of them – leaped up, grabbed their coats, and headed for the garage, or home, for shovels.

The Martini family arrived with shovels and a wheelbarrow. They shoveled as much snow as the wheelbarrow would hold, and then rolled it to the curb to dump it.

Makina Mwangi, calling Zuzu's cell phone for news of Marianne, learned of the need for shovelers. She promptly called her eleven-year-old son and told him to round up his friends and get to the church.

The Bishops and O'Briens came; so did the Randalls and Dr. Baldwin's family. Dr. Lin called his grown son and daughter, busily preparing the Chinese specialties they'd planned for dinner that night, and ordered them to go dig. Mr. Sanderson from the Building and Loan, who had forgotten he was wearing bedroom slippers, came to help.

Violet Bick's granddaughter Amy, in Bedford Falls to visit relatives, ran to the parking lot and began shoveling for all she was worth.

Jagan Chaudhury was just closing up his restaurant when he heard the news. He arrived with his young sons and began shoveling. Travis Gower, seeing the commotion on the street, went outside to find out what was going on.

"Let's go!" he told his assistant. They grabbed a dozen new shovels, which Gower Drugs carried this time of year, locked the door behind them, and ran to the church, passing out shovels to those who didn't have them. One of them was the Rev. Trevor Davis, who was shoving his arms into a battered pullover sweater as he ran down the street toward his church. Another was Dr. James Satinover, Mary's next-door neighbor. Jeremy Blake, who, thanks to Zuzu Bailey, had been buying Christmas gifts for his siblings, grabbed a shovel out of Travis Gower's hand and went to work.

Most of the townspeople hadn't bothered to put on coats or hats. They'd just grabbed their shovels and ran to the church after someone had called them or banged on their front doors and told them what had happened.

Within fifteen minutes, a third of the parking lot was cleared. Within twenty-five minutes, two-thirds.

Chapter 81
11 p.m.

Clarence took George's arm firmly.

"Hang on," he said.

The cold wind swirled around George once more. When he opened his eyes a few moments later, the rain had stopped, and he realized he was no longer in the city. He was standing on the sidewalk before a large Victorian house with a round turret. It was lit up with thousands of twinkle lights. An old-fashioned sleigh sat on the roof, with a realistic Santa guiding the reins of eight reindeer, which appeared to be pulling the sleigh skyward.

"Here we are," Clarence said. "We're going to visit the FitzGerald family."

George's heart was pounding. Was this the family he'd been contacted about, twenty years ago? The family whose son was in desperate need of –

"We can't just barge in on the family," Clarence said. "But I can get us both in, and they won't see us. We'll just observe for a while."

Clarence put his hand on George's back, and the two walked forward. When it appeared they would bang into the front door, George found himself walking through it, as though it were made of air.

It was one of the loveliest houses he'd ever seen, and he'd seen plenty. A mahogany staircase leading up to the second and third floors was decorated in greenery, red velvet ribbons, and white twinkle lights. On the left was a dining room, where a uniformed maid was removing the remains of a feast. To the right, in a living room with twelve-foot ceilings, stood a huge Christmas tree. Three small, giggling children had scooted on their backs as far under the tree as they could manage without knocking off baubles or hitting the trunk.

A woman in her late thirties, wearing a red plaid jacket over a long black velvet skirt, was passing out glasses of hot buttered rum to the others. A silver-haired man, who appeared to be in his seventies, was seated on the sofa, his arm around a woman of about the same age.

"Come and sit down, Heather," said a good-looking man of about forty. "You've done enough for one night."

The woman collapsed down next to him. "It's your turn, anyway, Charles. Time to read *The Night Before Christmas*."

The three children squealed with delight and hastily scooted out from beneath the tree.

"But first, go put on your pajamas and robes and slippers," Heather told them.

The children shot from the room. In less than two minutes, the children returned, panting and sweating and shouting "I win!" to each other.

"The book's on the coffee table," said Heather, smiling.

The children scrambled for the book and then ran to their father's lap. The youngest was left lapless.

"Come sit with me, sweetheart," her grandfather said, holding out his arms. The little girl climbed up the sofa, plopped down on her grandfather's lap, and rested her red head under his chin.

"'Twas the night before Christmas, and all through the house, not a creature was stirring, not even a mouse," their father began.

A log collapsed in the fireplace. The elderly woman got up to stir the fire.

"... When out on the lawn there arose such a clatter, I sprang from my bed to see what was the matter..."

It was a lovely sight. It was what every family should be at Christmas, George thought. Parents, children, grandparents, all under one roof. But the feeling of dread in his gut told him that what Clarence was about to say would be the worst of all the words and sights he'd endured this evening.

Clarence leaned closer to George. "This is the family that might have been. No, would have been," Clarence corrected himself, "if you had not been so selfish twenty years ago. If you had been willing to give up that trip to Europe – "

"When what to my wondering eyes should appear, but a miniature sleigh and eight tiny reindeer..."

Tears welled in George's eyes. He was shaking with fear, and with an awareness that he had done a great wrong to this family.

"That father over there, reading to his children," Clarence continued, "was the boy who needed that bone marrow transplant. Your bone marrow was a near perfect match. But the evening the Bone Marrow Registry called you, you were about to leave with your friends for a bicycling trip through Europe."

'Now Dasher, now Dancer, now Prancer and Vixen! On Comet, on Cupid, on Donder and Blitzen!'

"You'd been waiting a long time for that trip – "

"To the top of the porch, to the top of the wall – "

"You wanted to see the great art of Europe. It was the most important thing in the world to you..."

"So up to the house top the coursers they flew – "

"So you simply refused to donate your marrow. It would have meant you couldn't go to Europe..."

"His eyes, how they twinkled! His dimples, how merry!"

"... because even if you had delayed your trip by one day, and let the doctors remove your marrow, you would not have been in any shape to do any bicycling for at least a week – "

"He had a broad face and a little round belly, that shook when he laughed like a bowlful of jelly..."

"And in the end, you decided it just wasn't worth it."

"And laying his finger aside of his nose..."

"Those children over there – they don't exist," Clarence told him. "Those elderly grandparents – " George glanced again at the smiling couple seated on the sofa – "they died of grief when their only son died of leukemia at the age of eighteen."

"He sprang to his sleigh, to his team gave a whistle..."

George thought that nothing could be worse than this. He was wrong.

"The boy you refused to help," Clarence said. "Do you know what he would have done for a living? He was a brilliant young man. He'd have become a research scientist. He would have pioneered a cure for a disease that kills thousands of children every year, all over the world..."

"I thought – somebody else might – "

"And away they all flew like the down of a thistle..."

"But since he died twenty years ago, he naturally didn't find a cure," Clarence went on remorselessly. "And all the children he'd have saved over the years? They're all dead, too. He wasn't there to save them, because you were weren't there to save Charles."

"*Happy Christmas to all, and to all a good night!*"

Charles FitzGerald closed the book and kissed the two children in his lap.

"Time for bed now, or Santa Claus won't come!" he told them with a grin.

George Bailey could stand it no longer. Putting his hands over his face, he broke down and cried for the first time since his parents had died, twenty-six years before.

Chapter 82
11 p.m.

"Bundle her up well," Dr. Lin said.

The nurses wrapped two more blankets around Marianne, lying unconscious on the stretcher. They took her down on the elevator and out the emergency room door, where an ambulance waited. Carefully, they lifted her in.

The town's snowplows had started clearing streets again after the blizzard stopped, but they'd not had time to clear many by 11 p.m. Jack Higgins, a farmer who owned his own snowplow, had been texted about the emergency. He'd immediately come to town to plow the streets between the hospital and the Presbyterian Church. He was still plowing when nurses closed the ambulance door and the driver headed, slowly and carefully, to the church.

Chapter 83
11:13 p.m.

George knew he had been crying for several long minutes. But it was a cleansing cry. Clarence had led him, stumbling, through the walls of he FitzGerald home and then, slipping on the icy sidewalk, George had fallen, but was crying too hard to get himself up again.

That man. Those children. The Bradshaws and their little girl. All those children around the world who would have been saved. His own wife and children...

He thought of all his accomplishments: The company he'd founded, the buildings he'd built, or remodeled, the awards he had won, the immense amount of money he'd made. It all turned to ash in his mouth.

George reached for his handkerchief, wiped his eyes and blew his nose. Clarence sat quietly beside him, his wings nearly invisible.

"Is there... anything I can do to make things right?" George asked.

"If you mean, can you relive your life so things turn out differently, no," Clarence answered. "But if you mean you want to change your future, you can certainly do that."

"Amanda has left me."

"Amanda needs your love. She doesn't think she has it anymore. Neither do Peter and Marianne. If you make your family a priority, everything will be all right in the end, I promise you."

"And the little Bradshaw girl. Will she live?"

Clarence looked uncomfortable. "I'm not supposed to tell you that."

"Please, Clarence! I've had enough to deal with for one night."

Clarence sighed. "All right, George. I'll tell you. Gracie has a long, hard haul ahead of her, but she's going to be all right. And so will her brother and her mother."

"Thank God for that."

"And her father is going to sue you."

"Well, that's not surprising," George said bleakly. He got to his feet, put away his handkerchief, and looked around.

"Can we go back to the real world, now? I still need to visit my grandmother, and I want to get back to my wife and kids."

"Not yet, George." Clarence took hold of George's arm as the two began to walk down the street. "I have a few more things to teach you."

"I'm listening, Clarence."

"Good. First of all, Bedford Falls needs your attention."

"You mean, I should move back here?" Even in his misery, George shuddered at the thought of having to move back to a small town.

"No, George, you don't have to move there. Your work is in New York. But you should not have forgotten Bedford Falls, the town you grew up in – the town your family has sacrificed so much for."

Clarence reached behind himself and massaged his back.

"Lord, I'm stiff," he muttered. "I've been down here in the cold a long time. Anyway – back to Bedford Falls. All towns need somebody strong enough to protect them. In the early part of the last century, your great-grandfather did this. And when he died, your grandfather took over, making sure poor people were not victimized by a vicious old man who cared more about piling up money than – "

George winced.

" – than he did about people.

"He saved his little brother from drowning at the cost of half his hearing. He gave up his chance of college to save his father's vision of creating decent homes for decent people. He gave up his honeymoon money to protect the town from Henry Potter's evil mechanisms. He was prepared to take the blame for the money his Uncle Billy lost. And when, after twenty years of sacrifice, when he inherited Potter's money, what did he do? He spent most of it on the town."

"But my grandfather wanted to get away from Bedford Falls," George said. "He spent twenty miserable years toiling away at a job he hated. It's all in the story. He had so many gifts. If Old Man Potter hadn't left him all that money, he'd never have had a chance to use them."

"You're forgetting something, George," Clarence responded. "You live in a fallen world. Bad things happen. Your grandfather's father, Peter

Bailey, died earlier than he should have because of the stress Potter put on him. That had repercussions that affected your grandfather."

Clarence adjusted his hat and continued down the sidewalk with George.

"And you have to remember, your grandfather lived during the Great Depression. A great many people had gifts they were never able to use because there wasn't money to send them to college. Or their fathers died and their mothers had to work, and they had to take care of their younger siblings instead of going to college."

Clarence peered up into George's face.

"Your grandfather learned early on that it's possible to turn what people like Mr. Potter intend for evil, into something good. Potter tried over and over again to destroy the Building and Loan, and all the good it was doing for the people of Bedford Falls. He tried to do it on the day your grandfather was planning to leave for college. He tried to do it on the day your grandparents got married. He tried to do it when he offered George a job that would have forced him to abandon the Building and Loan. And he tried to do it the day your Uncle Billy lost that $8,000.

"Each time Potter tried to inflict evil on the town, your grandfather turned it into something good. Yes, he did it at great personal sacrifice, but sometimes sacrifice is what's required of us in a fallen world."

Clarence tightened his scarf around his neck.

"We simply have to do the best we can in the situation we find ourselves in. We need to remember that our families, our friends, our communities – and yes, even strangers and generations yet unborn – have claims on us. Your Great-Uncle Billy, for instance – "

George remembered the stories of Uncle Billy. He'd always thought Great-grandfather had to have been crazy to go into business with him.

"There you go again," Clarence said irritably. "Of course Peter Bailey could have chosen a better business partner. The point is, he knew Billy needed taking care of, and he was willing to do it. It meant he had to work harder, of course, since Billy was not very bright. But Billy had a happy life, and that counted for a lot in Peter Bailey's book. Which brings me to your Uncle Tommy."

Chapter 84
11:13 p.m.

The moon rose over Bedford Falls, its light shining down into the noisy church parking lot as the townspeople continued to dig as fast as they could. By 11:15, three quarters of the parking lot was cleared. More people arrived to grab the shovels out of the hands of exhausted diggers and began pitching snow into wheelbarrows themselves.

Chapter 85
11:15 p.m.

"What about Uncle Tommy?" George asked. He had always felt the same sense of impatience with Tommy as he had with Billy, the great-great-uncle he knew only through stories.

"Tommy can't help it that he doesn't have the fine mind you have," Clarence said softly. "And don't give yourself credit for being smart: You were born with intellectual gifts, just as Tommy was born without them. You didn't do anything to earn them, so you might as well stop being so darned proud of them. And remember, the Lord values each of us equally."

The pair turned a corner and continued walking.

"My point is," Clarence said, "you have to look after family members who don't have the gifts you do. How do you think Tommy feels about being the only one in his family who didn't succeed? He knows what you think of him, by the way."

George winced again.

"So you want me to help Uncle Tommy?"

Clarence sighed. "Well, somebody needs to help him." He took off his hat, shook off the snow, and put it back on his head.

"When we get back to Bedford Falls, I want you to take a good look around you. Old Man Potters have slithered back into Bedford Falls, and if somebody like you doesn't do something soon, everything your grandfather worked and sacrificed for will be gone, probably forever.

"So – " Clarence finished, "Imagine how your grandfather and your great-grandfather would have seen things. And then, use your brains and your money and your experience and your family heritage to *do* something, before it's too late."

"Is that all?" George asked, kicking a clump of snow out of his way.

"Not quite," Clarence answered. "Remember when I talked about the fallen world a minute ago?"

"Yes, I remember."

"Did you ever wonder how that fallenness affected you?"

George thought of his good health, his ability to make money, his beautiful wife, his son and daughter. "No," he finally responded. "I guess I never did."

"What about your mother and father dying in that plane crash?"

George stiffened.

"What about it?"

"Think about how *that* affected you," Clarence said softly.

The clouds had now dispersed, and a few stars appeared in the dark sky. Clarence stopped and turned to face George.

"You lost your ability to trust that day," he said quietly. "You lost your belief that life would treat you fairly. In a way, your loss was worse than your grandfather's not being able to go to college, or on a honeymoon, or to work at a job that made full use of his gifts."

Clarence stopped and turned to look George full in the face.

"Why? Because you started trusting money instead. You thought if you just had enough money, you could protect yourself from life's horrors. And the more you made, the more you craved. The more you had – your wife, your children – the more frightened you became. So you spent all your time and all your energy piling up money – walls of money that would protect you and your family.

"But it didn't work, did it?"

George put his hands to his face again. Clarence looked at him sympathetically.

"We're going back now, George. Back to Bedford Falls – and back to the rest of your life. Make the most of it."

A rush of wind swept over George, blurring his vision for a few moments. And then he found himself standing alone next to his damaged SUV, still parked by the police station.

Chapter 86
11:17 p.m.

George looked around. Clarence was definitely gone. People were running up and down the street, shouting something about shovels. George was puzzled. Had someone fallen into a snowbank? Somebody grabbed his arm. George turned around. It was Aunt Zuzu.

"George! I can't believe you're here!" Zuzu gasped.

"What's going on?" George asked, alarmed. He'd never seen Aunt Zuzu looking so upset.

"Oh, George..." Zuzu swallowed hard. "Marianne ran into the street and – she was hit by a car."

Zuzu could not face telling George whose car it was that had run over his little girl. "She's in the hospital, but she needs to be flown to a trauma center."

Zuzu watched George's face as he absorbed these shocks, and then gestured to the lit-up church parking lot on the next block, where dozens of people were frantically shoveling snow.

"We need to clear a space big enough for the helicopter to land – "

George began to run.

Chapter 87
11:19 p.m.

Roberto Martini threw a load of snow onto the wheelbarrow and paused, gasping for breath. The old man was near exhaustion, but refused to give up. Suddenly, a tall man raced into the lot and grabbed Roberto Martini's shovel. Martini stared as the man swiftly scooped up a huge load of snow and dumped it in the wheelbarrow.

George Bailey, Mary's grandson and Marianne's father, had arrived at last.

Chapter 88
11:20 p.m.

An ambulance containing Marianne, Amanda, and medics arrived and parked next to the church. They did not have long to wait. The sound of helicopter blades whirring in the night sounded above them. The townspeople shoveled faster, clearing the last of the snow from the parking lot. Moments later, they could see the copter approaching.

"Get out of the way!" Roberto Martini shouted.

The shovelers ran from the lot and looked up. The noise of the blades was much louder now as the copter wavered overhead and then slowly began its descent. At 11:25 p.m. exactly, it landed.

George ran to the ambulance.

"Amanda!"

George feared what he would see in his wife's face. But when a startled Amanda looked up at her husband, her blue eyes showed nothing but relief. She fell into his arms.

The paramedics carried Marianne out on a stretcher. George and Amanda walked on either side of their unconscious daughter to the helicopter. The medics placed her carefully into the copter, along with her medical gear, and hopped aboard themselves. So did George and Amanda.

The people of Bedford Falls, exhausted and perspiring, stood watching as the helicopter lifted and swung northwest toward Rochester. Moments later, even the sound of the blades had faded into the darkness.

Chapter 89
11:25 p.m.

The citizens of Bedford Falls now jammed their shovels into the heaped-up snow and went inside the church. Tired as they were, they knew their jobs were not yet done.

They had carefully planned a lovely Christmas Eve service. But that service was not to be. Instead, the citizens of Bedford Falls, wearing jeans and boots and sweaters in place of their Christmas finery, dropped to their knees to pray for Marianne.

Janie, gratefully watching her neighbors, wondered if she should play something on the organ. She also wondered where Roberto and the boys had disappeared to. She saw her sister near the front, her head bent as she prayed, and thought about that Christmas Eve, sixty-two years ago, when the whole family, and most of the townspeople, was praying for Daddy. Once again, the entire town had pulled off a miracle for the Bailey family. *That is, if Marianne survives*, Janie thought.

At the back of the church, in the last pew, Janie saw her great-nephew Peter. He had manfully shoveled snow with the rest of them, and now, alone and apparently forgotten, the boy was trying hard not to cry as he thought of his injured sister.

Janie's eyes shifted to the other side of the church. Her brother Tommy was also in the back, his head down, his chubby hands folded on the pew ahead of him. Her heart went out to him. Dear, sweet Tommy, who was so like Uncle Billy.

Janie walked up the aisle to the back of the sanctuary, and wrapped her arms around Peter. As the boy reached up to put his arms around her, Janie felt silent sobs shake his body. She held him comfortingly for a minute or two until he was able to calm down. As he settled back in his pew, wiping his face, Janie smiled at him and gave his shoulder a final pat.

Then she walked across the aisle to the other back pew, and sat next to Tommy, putting a hand on top of his. He paused in his prayers long enough to look up and see who it was. Janie smiled at him, too, and patted his arm.

"That was a great idea you had," she whispered.

But Tommy was not comforted. He put his head down on his hands and continued his prayers for Marianne.

Chapter 90
11:25 p.m.

As the helicopter cut through the dark skies, George reached out to touch Marianne's hand. He had not prayed in years, but now he prayed fervently, "God, please save Marianne. Please let her be all right."

Like most people who didn't pray often, George kept repeating himself. And in desperation, he prayed, "God, I'll do anything if you will only save Marianne. I'll give away all my money. I'll let those poor people stay in my building. I'll be a better father."

George knew he was treating God the way he treated those with whom he did business: You do this for me, and I'll do this for you. But he didn't know how else to pray.

Thirty minutes later, the helicopter landed on the roof of St. Elizabeth's. The medics carefully lifted Marianne out and took her into the elevator. Downstairs, a surgical team awaited her.

Chapter 91
11:35 p.m.

The Reverend Trevor Davis stood up. Instead of his usual ministerial robes, he was wearing jeans wet to the knees and a bright green Christmas sweater decorated with a reindeer. He walked to the front of the altar, and waited. One by one, parishioners looked up.

"Thank you all for being here, tonight," Davis began. "This has been a very unusual Christmas Eve service. But in a way, I think it's the greatest one we've ever had. Coming to the rescue of a little girl, and praying for her survival – this is what the church is all about. It's what community is all about," he added hastily as he caught sight of friends from other faiths and denominations, and a few with no faith, in the pews before him.

"Jesus said, 'Inasmuch as you have done it to one of the least of these my brethren, you have done it to me,'" he continued. "All of you have served the Christ Child tonight."

He looked around the pews again, and smiled, silently praying for guidance.

"What I'd like to do now is light some candles, sing a few hymns, and then have a final group prayer for Marianne Bailey. Does that sound all right to you?"

The congregation murmured its assent. The minister motioned to a few of the young people to come over to him. "Would you please light the candles on the altar?" he asked.

He caught Janie's eye. She came forward and sat down in her usual place at the church organ. She softly began playing "I Pray on Christmas," a newer song that seemed highly appropriate tonight. The congregation had been rehearsing it so they would know it on Christmas Eve.

After running through the melody once, Janie nodded to the congregation. They began to sing.

> *I pray on Christmas*
> *Oh, the sick will soon be strong*
> *'I pray on Christmas*
> *The Lord will hear my song.*

At the conclusion of this song, Janie began a more familiar one.

> *Oh, holy night!*
> *The Stars are brightly shining,*
> *It is the night of our dear Savior's birth*
> *Long lay the world in sin and error pining,*
> *'Til He appear'd and the soul felt its worth...*

The candlelight flickered softly on the faces of the congregation and lit the white walls and dark walnut pews of the old sanctuary. How she loved these dear people, Zuzu thought.

Janie launched into "Silent Night." And then the Rev. Davis came forward again.

"Let us pray," he said. The congregation bowed their heads.

Above them, the church bells tolled twelve times. It was midnight.

Tuesday, December 25, 2007

Chapter 92
12:10 a.m.

At St. Elizabeth's Hospital, a team of doctors, including Angela Grant, a neurosurgeon who had hastily left a family poker game when her beeper went off, worked feverishly over the little girl who'd been brought to them so badly injured.

Dr. Grant thought of her own daughter, five-year-old Penelope. By now, Angela's husband would have tucked Penny safely into bed to await Santa Claus's visit. Dr. Grant did not know the Bailey family, but she knew this little girl must be special to someone.

God, help us to save her, she prayed.

Chapter 93
12:10 a.m.

As prayers for Marianne Bailey ended, Roberto Martini and his sons entered the back door of the sanctuary.

"We've brought some refreshments from the restaurant," Roberto announced. "Hot cider, tortellini bolognese, lasagna, garlic bread, and cranberry cheesecake."

Chapter 94

The sun rose over Bedford Falls at 7:18 a.m, on an eighteen-degree Christmas morning. The snowplows had already been running for hours. In a little while, the neighborhood's children would undoubtedly burst outside to try out new sleds, but now, all was peaceful.

In Rochester, George Bailey, slumped over in a chair in the hospital waiting room, opened his eyes. He'd snatched perhaps an hour of sleep that night. In the chair next to him, Amanda stirred.

Looking up, George saw Dr. Grant filling out paperwork at the nurses' station. She had been up all night monitoring her little patient. George got up and went to the counter.

"How's she doing?" he asked.

Dr. Grant put her pen back in the pocket of her white coat.

"She's still unconscious," she replied. "But she's got a good chance if she wakes up soon. Would you like to see her?"

George wakened Amanda and the two followed the doctor down the hall and entered Marianne's room in the intensive care unit. Looking down at his daughter, George saw a little girl whose head was wrapped in bandages. Her face was swollen, and she was still hooked up to machines. But she was alive.

George sat down in the chair next to Marianne's bed. Amanda dragged over another chair and sat next to him. They prayed, and waited.

Chapter 95

At Mary Bailey's house, Zuzu had risen early despite being up so late the night before. She put on her old, green-and-gold plaid robe, checked on Mary, and made coffee. She drank it while standing at the living room window, watching a cardinal hop from the fence to a nearby tree. A Christmas gift from nature, she thought.

At 7:30 a.m., Zuzu called Amanda's cell phone to check on Marianne. As she did so, Janie came down the stairs to grab a cup of coffee. Moments later, they heard the sound of bare feet charging down the living room stairs. Half a dozen young Baileys raced into the kitchen. Seeing Zuzu on the phone, they waited.

"Give George my love," Zuzu said. "We'll miss you today, but we can make it up when you and Marianne get home."

She clicked off her phone.

"They're waiting for Marianne to wake up," she reported. "If she wakes up soon, she'll probably be okay."

Janie hugged Zuzu comfortingly.

"Can we open our presents now?" seven-year-old Benjamin asked, hopping up and down in the still-chilly air.

"Go put your bathrobe and slippers on first," Zuzu told him, smiling.

Chapter 96

At 10:17 a.m., Marianne opened her eyes. Looking around her, she saw her mother and father sitting nearby, apparently asleep. She was in a strange bed, in a strange room. Her head hurt. The last thing she remembered was sitting in a rocking chair at Grandma Mary's house, trying not to cry because Daddy wasn't there.

But Daddy *was* here.

"Daddy?" she whispered.

George Bailey opened his eyes.

"Marianne," he breathed.

He reached over to touch her cheek. "My little love."

Chapter 97

By late afternoon, Zuzu and Janie were exhausted. Tommy, who'd built a fire in the big living room fireplace, was now carefully gathering up torn wrapping paper and ribbon and feeding the flames with them.

The younger children had gone to a nearby hill for sledding, and while they were out of the way, the women had turned the leftovers from the night before into a Christmas lunch.

Janie entertained the children by urging them to choose Christmas carols for her to play on the piano. She played them crazily, making them laugh and pound on the piano themselves.

"Too loud!" Zuzu warned them. "Grandma Mary is trying to rest."

Janie put a look of extreme shame on her face, making the children laugh again. Zuzu rolled her eyes.

They had all been goofy with happiness since George had called with the good news. But enough was enough.

"I'd better go check on Mother," she said, putting down her cup of tea and getting up.

Zuzu walked down the hall to her mother's room, opened the door, and peeked in.

"Mother?"

The room was lit only by a lamp by the bed. Everything was quiet.

"Are you sleeping, mother?"

Zuzu tiptoed over to Mary's bed.

"Mother?"

Taking a closer look at her mother's face in the dim light, Zuzu gasped.

Chapter 98

George sat in the hospital chapel, his elbows on his knees, his head down. Thinking back over his life, he could remember several prayers in which he had asked God for something. But this was the first time he had ever thanked Him for anything.

Amanda was with Marianne. George was glad to be alone. He needed to think about what had happened the night before, after he'd hit that bridge.

He knew that great changes were in store for him, and for his family. He would have much hard work to do, repairing the damage he had done over the years. He knew he couldn't go back and fix things, as Clarence had reminded him. But then, nobody could. In a fallen world, everyone made mistakes. All one could do was apologize, ask forgiveness, and try to do better.

George knew he had a lot to learn about loving people. Amanda would help him with that. So would the example of his grandparents.

The door to the chapel softly opened. George turned around. It was Amanda, a worried look on her face. He was instantly on his feet.

"What's wrong?" he asked, fear gripping his heart.

"Marianne is doing okay," she answered. "But George – I just got a call from Zuzu. She said your grandmother keeps lapsing into unconsciousness. Dr. Baldwin is with her. He says Mary has just a few hours left."

Amanda looked up at him sorrowfully. "I'm so sorry, darling."

"I should have gone to see her," George said. He dropped back down onto a pew. "Why didn't I go see her? Now, I'll never see her again."

Amanda put her hand on his shoulder.

"Maybe you can," she said tentatively.

"No, Amanda, I can't leave you and Marianne."

"George, Marianne is doing fine. I'll stay with her. But I want you to go see Mary, before it's too late."

George thought about how he'd almost lost his daughter.

"No, Amanda. I want to stay here with Marianne."

Amanda smiled.

"You don't know how much it means to me to hear you say that," she said softly. "But she's going to be okay. You can go see Mary and then come right back."

George hesitated. "Are you sure that's what you want?"

"I'm sure."

The couple embraced tightly, and then George left. As he pulled out his cell phone to arrange for a private plane to fly him back to Bedford Falls, he suddenly remembered the words Clarence had spoken the night before.

We need to remember that our families, our friends, our communities – and yes, even strangers and generations as yet unborn – have claims on us...

So many strangers – at least, strangers to George – had worked mightily to save Marianne last night, digging out that parking lot. He could never thank them enough.

Chapter 99

Janie, Zuzu, and Tommy sat with their mother in her dimly lit bedroom in the old Bailey house. Dr. Baldwin sat on the other side of the room, not wanting to intrude, but wanting to stay with Mary Bailey until the end.

Mary's breathing was erratic, and she turned her head from side to side restlessly. She opened her eyes and stared at her children.

"Where's George?" Mary asked.

Janie and Zuzu looked at each other.

"Does she mean Daddy?" Janie whispered.

Mary closed her eyes again.

Amanda had phoned from the hospital to say that Mary's grandson was on his way. Zuzu fought against the bitterness she felt toward her nephew, who had worried Mary so much in her final year, and had refused to come visit her. She prayed that he would make it in time.

Nobody had told Mary about Marianne's accident. She had been upset enough about the collapse of the McClure building.

As Mary began to mutter, Zuzu reached out to take her blue-veined hand. *She is the last of her generation*, she thought sadly. *Daddy and Uncle Harry and Aunt Ruth and Uncle Marty are all gone. Now, Janie and Tommy and I will be the oldest Baileys.*

It was a strange feeling. Zuzu could remember her childhood so vividly. How was it possible that she was now so old? How could her adorable baby brother be in his sixties?

She listened to the soft sounds of the house. The younger children were asleep, the older ones talking quietly in the living room. Grandchildren, great-grandchildren, nieces and nephews and Hatch relatives had tiptoed in one by one to kiss Mary goodbye.

In the kitchen, Gabriela and her three daughters were washing dishes and putting away the silver.

Mary's silver.

Janie's son Ed was outside, shoveling the snow off Mary's walkway despite the lateness of the hour, needing something to do.

Zuzu did not hear the soft knock on the front door. But she did hear the sound of it being opened. A minute later, Gabriela pushed open the door to Mary's room. Zuzu, Janie, Tommy, and Dr. Baldwin looked up.

"George is here," she whispered.

Chapter 100

George Bailey, still wearing his coat, stepped quietly into Mary's bedroom. Zuzu silently got to her feet and let him take the chair closest to Mary.

George sat down and took his grandmother's warm hand in his cold one. He heard the rattling sound of her sigh.

"Grandmother?" he said softly. "It's George."

Mary sighed again.

"George," she whispered. She gasped for air.

She's going! Zuzu thought fearfully.

Mary opened her eyes and looked at George.

"I... prayed... for you," she whispered. ' 'I know," George said. He wanted Mary, and Mary alone, to understand what had happened to him on Christmas Eve. He bent down closer, looking directly into her faded blue eyes. He gently squeezed her hand.

"I know you prayed," he whispered in her ear. "Clarence told me."

A faint smile played on Mary's lips. Very faintly, she squeezed his hand back and looked lovingly into his eyes – the eyes so like those of her late husband. *Everything will be all right now*, she thought sleepily.

"Goodbye, Grandmother," George said, his voice catching. "I love you."

Mary did not hear him. Faint music was playing somewhere far away.

Buffalo gals can't you come out tonight, can't you come out tonight, can't you come out tonight...

As the loving faces around her faded away, Mary heard her name being called, as if from a great distance.

"Mary!"

It was George. She tried to say his name, but no longer had the strength.

"She's going," Dr. Baldwin said quietly.

George's voice came again, closer this time.

"Hey, Mary!"

She saw him as he appeared over a grassy hill, running towards her – young, as he was on the night of Harry's high school graduation dance.

George Bailey, I'll love you 'til the day I die...

He was closer now. In another minute, she would be in his arms.

"Mary!"

Mary's family, gathered around her bed, saw a tiny smile crease her face. As she faded out of one life and into the next, Mary felt herself becoming young again.

"I'm coming, George..."

Epilogue

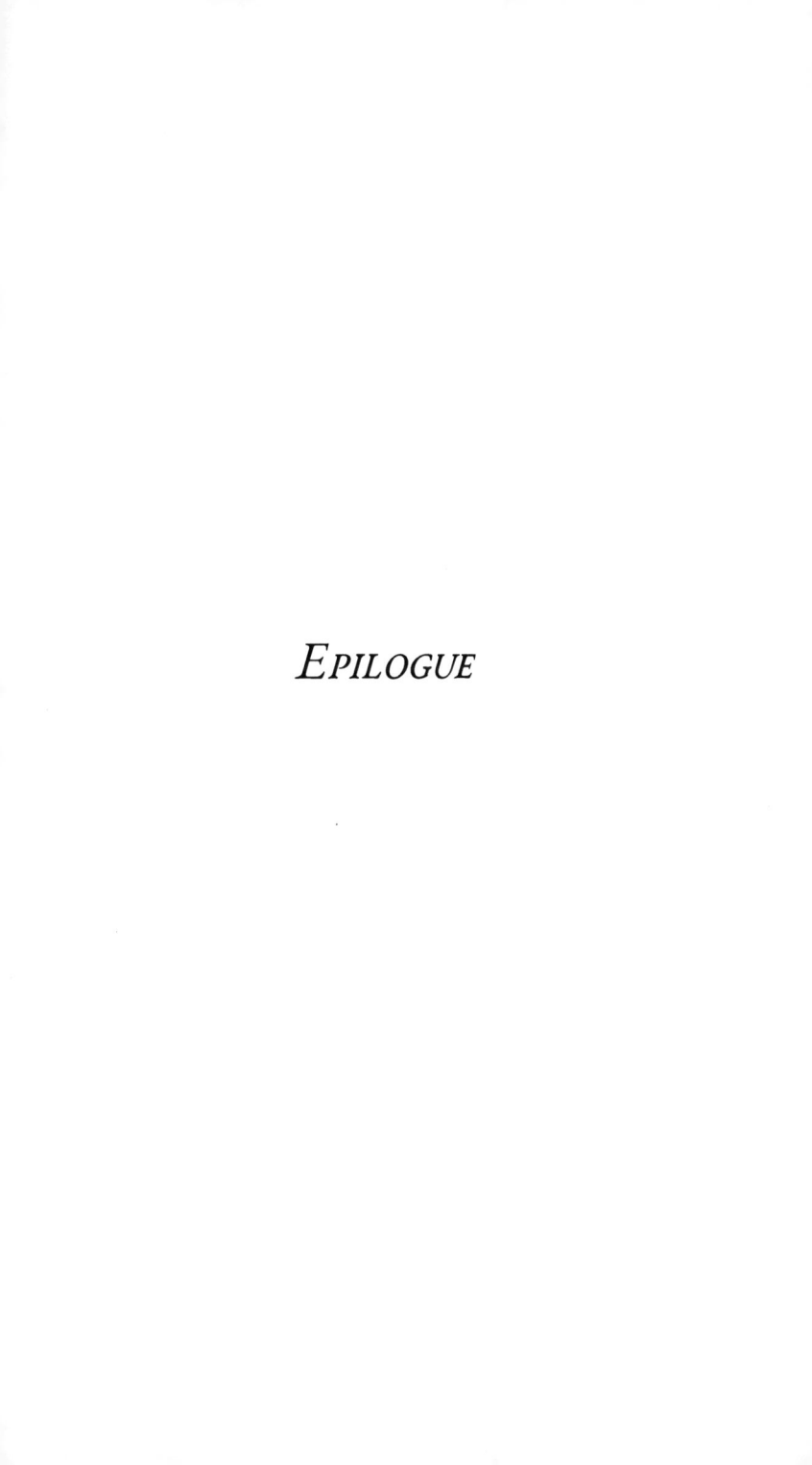

Christmas, 2014

The year following Christmas of 2007 was a difficult one for George Bailey, but he kept the promises he'd made to himself as he sat beside his little daughter at St. Elizabeth's Hospital, waiting to learn if she would live or die.

When Uncle Tommy came to George and Amanda to beg their forgiveness, they both embraced him and told him they forgave him, and that they loved him, which made Tommy cry.

The family of Olivia Bradshaw sued Bailey Investments; George settled out of court for ten million dollars. George apologized in person to the Bradshaws and visited them frequently as they recovered from their injuries. If they could not fully forgive him for the harm he'd done their family, they did recognize that he was a changed man.

George also dealt with New York prosecutors who looked closely into the circumstances that had led to the collapse of the McClure building's seventh floor. They ordered Bailey Investments to pay a large fine and perform the necessary repairs to the building, making it safe for future occupants.

Brian Fulmer, hoping to avoid jail time, cut a deal with prosecutors, telling them of the man on the city planning commission who had accepted bribes over the years to overlook shoddy work. He was arrested, and served a prison term.

George followed his niece Kayla's advice regarding Trent Towers. He announced that all those who had been forced out could return to their apartments and live out their lives there. In the meantime, he made many improvements to the building. When families returned, George knocked on their doors and offered each of them a big basket of fruit and an apology. A little girl named Leticia threw her arms around his knees in thanks.

George began spending a great deal of time with his children, letting them know they were the most important people in his life. When Marianne was given a role in another school play, her father sat in the front row so she could see him. He also turned up at every one of Peter's football games, sitting in the stands with Amanda to cheer him on.

George and Amanda continued to live in New York City, but spent much more time in Bedford Falls. George had learned many things on that Christmas Eve of 2007, among them that to whom much is given, from him much is expected. George now took a hard look at what had gone wrong with Bedford Falls. And then he set about setting things right, and did so with relish, just as his grandfather had done.

First, he offered enough money to the owners of the two bars that they agreed to sell their properties to him and move elsewhere. They were encouraged to accept his offer by his promise to make life very difficult for them if they refused to leave. Given that Tommy Bailey had imbibed at both bars on Christmas Eve, leading to the accident that had harmed George Bailey's daughter, this was a wise decision. As for the men's club, George offered the owner enough money to convince him, not only to close down, but to agree never to open a similar business elsewhere, thereby ensuring that there would be one less grubby business in the world.

George spent a considerable sum upgrading the Bedford Falls hospital into a first-class facility. He added an underground heating system to the heliport to make it easier for patients to be taken to big-city hospitals in winter when necessary.

George missed his grandmother deeply, as did the other Baileys. But he was comforted by the knowledge that she had lived the life she had wanted to live ever since she had first fallen in love with George's grandfather as a little girl.

As for Tommy Bailey, George tried to make up for many years of neglect. George realized that Tommy, like Uncle Billy, needed an extra portion of love and understanding from his family. He also needed work to make him feel useful. George encouraged Tommy to enter an alcohol rehab center, which Tommy – still guilty over what he'd done to George's daughter – agreed to do. George then created and funded the George and Mary Bailey Foundation, designed to protect the Bailey family legacy and fund projects that would improve the lives of the people of Bedford Falls. George made Tommy one of the trustees, along with Zuzu and Janie.

George also gave Tommy a part-time job at the Building and Loan to make sure hard-working families like the Cruzes and the Mwangis and the Tuckers – the people who did most of the working and paying and living and dying in Bedford Falls – could raise their children in decent homes.

George did not know it, but every night, his Uncle Tommy knelt down beside his bed and tearfully prayed a prayer of thanksgiving for the nephew who had done so much to make his life worth living.

Whenever he was in Bedford Falls, George attended the Presbyterian church downtown. The Reverend Davis, cannily recognizing that George Bailey had become a force for good in the town, told him of the gambling addiction some of the townspeople suffered from. George, working with the town council, encouraged the local grocery stores to remove their lottery machines. When some of them protested – the games were moneymakers, after all – George sent Tommy Bailey as a convincer. Tommy explained that the George and Mary Bailey Family Foundation planned to buy Thanksgiving, Christmas, and Easter dinners for the poor of Bedford Falls, and would purchase food only at stores free of lottery games.

Knowing they were beaten – and a little fearful of what crazy idea George Bailey might come up with next – the store owners complied. At George's suggestion, the Bailey Family Foundation let it be known that it would pay for treatment for any Bedford Fallsians who had become addicted to gambling.

The sister of Charles FitzGerald never discovered the name of the anonymous donor who created and funded the Charles FitzGerald Bone Cancer Research Center. But she was grateful that someone remembered her brother, all these years later.

Much to the chagrin of his New York friends, George never again wrote a big check to a city art museum. But he did keep an eye out for promising young artists in Bedford Falls. The Bailey Family Foundation loaned them money to attend art schools; some of them repaid their debt by creating art for Bedford Falls' public spaces.

George met Dr. Joshua Purdue one morning at Redeemer Presbyterian Church in New York, where he and Amanda and the kids now faithfully worshipped. George didn't exactly like him, but he did give money to support the doctor's missions of mercy.

The citizens of Bedford Falls grew to love George Bailey, just as they had loved his grandfather. Bedford Falls would never be perfect – no town could be in a fallen world – but George made sure it was the best place to live that money, attention, and love could create. And for the first time in his life, George Bailey understood the meaning of genuine friendship, and became a true friend to many.

Mary had left the old Bailey house to George, who allowed Aunt Zuzu to live in her childhood home for the rest of her life. Every summer, George brought Amanda and the children to Bedford Falls to renew friendships, deepen family ties, and enjoy the little town five generations of Baileys had loved and lived in. For even Mary's great-grandchildren were now finding ways to volunteer their time to better the town, and protect it.

George also brought his family to Bedford Falls every Christmas. On Christmas Eve, they worshiped at the Presbyterian Church, where they listened to Janie play the ancient carols on the organ. Roberto Martini and his children and grandchildren prepared a huge feast for the Baileys, Hatches, and Martinis. And then the old house on 320 Sycamore rang far into the night with song, joy, and laughter.

By Christmas of 2014, George and Amanda had welcomed two more babies into their family, both born near Christmas: a girl they named Noelle and a son – born two days previously in the Bedford Falls Hospital – whom George wanted to name Clarence.

"Why on earth do you want to name him Clarence?" Amanda asked, picking up the squalling infant. "It's such an old-fashioned name. And nobody in our families is named Clarence."

George smiled down at the sight of his beautiful wife nursing his newborn son.

"I just like it," he said. He glanced upward at the portrait of an angel he'd commissioned – a strange, elderly, white-haired angel with a fine set of wings – and winked.

Acknowledgments

I wish to thank my husband, Brent Morse, for his help with medical and construction details, and for catching various oddities and impossibilities when he read the manuscript. I also want to thank Roberto Rivera, a colleague and friend, for his assistance with New York City details.

Kim Moreland, thank you for creating the family trees – a difficult task, as I kept changing the names of characters. Rachael Sinclair, your cover art is magnificent! Gina Dalfonzo, thank you for all kinds of assistance, including editing the manuscript for me.

Michael Willian's book, *It's A Wonderful Life: A Scene-by-Scene Guide to the Classic Film*, was extremely helpful, particularly the maps of Bedford Falls.

A big thank you to Frank Capra, who took a little Christmas story and turned it into an unforgettable film.

Following are verses that inspired the writing of Bedford Falls:

"Do not be overcome by evil, but overcome evil with good."
Romans 12:21

"You intended to harm me, but God intended it for good to accomplish what is now being done, the saving of many lives."
Genesis 50:20

"And to whomsoever much is given, of him much shall be required."
Luke 12:48

Printed in Great Britain
by Amazon